GERALDINE'S WAR

Sequel to MY DARLING GERALDINE

It is four years since Geraldine Wyllie's beloved husband, Laurence, died. He had gradually weakened over the years, due to injuries sustained in the First World War. Since his death, Geraldine had drawn closer to his parents, and she had been kept busy with her three children and with the work of the Kinloch Trust. During the difficult years of the Second World War, two men fall in love with Geraldine: the actor Richard Ransome, a childhood friend; and Alex Kinloch, Laurence's surgeon . . .

Books by Jane Carrick
in the Linford Romance Library:

DIAMONDS ON THE LAKE
A PEARL FOR LOVE
A HANDFUL OF MIST
THE COURAGE OF ANNA CAMERON
FACE OF A STRANGER
MY DARLING GERALDINE

JANE CARRICK

GERALDINE'S WAR

Sequel to
MY DARLING GERALDINE

Complete and Unabridged

LINFORD
Leicester

First published in Great Britain in 1986

First Linford Edition
published 2004

British Library CIP Data

Carrick, Jane
    Geraldine's war.—Large print ed.—
Linford romance library
    1. Love stories
    2. Large type books
    I. Title
    823.9′14 [F]

    ISBN 1–84395–361–7

Published by
F. A. Thorpe (Publishing)
Anstey, Leicestershire

Set by Words & Graphics Ltd.
Anstey, Leicestershire
Printed and bound in Great Britain by
T. J. International Ltd., Padstow, Cornwall

This book is printed on acid-free paper

Lost For Words

Geraldine Wyllie spent a few more minutes checking her appearance in the full-length mirror while she waited for the taxi to take her to the station.

The committee meeting in Edinburgh of the Kinloch Trust was to be a special one. The Trust had been founded exactly ten years previously in 1926 by Geraldine and Laurence Wyllie in order to benefit the work of Dr Alexander Kinloch.

How it had grown over the years, Geraldine mused, as she smoothed down the heavy silk skirt of her suit and checked that the seams of her pure silk fully-fashioned stockings were straight. She had bought the suit in Paris a few months before, liking the bright, vivid, raspberry red colour described as 'Framboise.'

Then she carefully pinned her halo

hat on top of her neatly-set hair and picked up her matching gloves and handbag before making her way downstairs.

Her mother-in-law, Constance Wyllie, was sitting beside the fire in the large drawing-room whilst her father-in-law, Stephen Wyllie, sat near the window, concentrating on a crossword. Old Mrs Wyllie suffered badly from arthritis, but she hadn't allowed it to spoil her sweet nature. She would be seventy in a few more days, and the family were already planning a birthday party for her.

'You look lovely, Geraldine dear,' she said as the younger woman walked into the room.

'Thank you.' Geraldine smiled, then turned enquiring eyes towards her father-in-law, who regarded her rather more critically as he cleared his throat. He and Geraldine argued over many things from what was best for her three children to the international situation, but they both secretly enjoyed these heated discussions, and rarely argued with anger.

The death of Geraldine's husband, Laurence, in 1932, had brought Geraldine very close to his parents, and in the four years since then they had treated one another with love and respect.

'There's the taxi,' Geraldine told them. 'I might be a little late since I'm catching the last train from Edinburgh.'

*   *   *

Alex Kinloch was eagerly waiting for her at Waverley Station. He had liked and admired Laurence Wyllie very much and had tried his best to prolong Laurence's good health. But his war wounds had sapped his strength. Geraldine had been inconsolable for a while, then she had squared her shoulders and thrown herself once again into the turmoil of life, helping to raise a great deal of money so that other people could have the benefit of the best treatment possible, as had Laurence.

Alex had always admired her, but never more so than this evening as he escorted her into the hotel where the other committee members, wives and friends, had all assembled to greet her.

Geraldine was soon listening closely to the treasurer's report which was very satisfactory, and later to the chairman's report on future plans for the trust. Then her cheeks grew warm with colour as she was presented with a lovely gold watch, inscribed on the back, for the work she had put into the trust.

'Mrs Wyllie,' the chairman reminded them, 'is still our president and we hope she will continue to carry on with this good work for a great many years.'

Later, after the committee meeting had broken up and the members had enjoyed a cup of tea and a few sandwiches, Alex Kinloch checked his own watch.

'We have an hour yet before your train leaves, Geraldine,' he said, 'and it's only ten minutes to the station.

Would you care to sit with me in the lounge for a little while? I'll order us a drink.'

'Oh dear,' Geraldine laughed. 'I hope nobody from Fairlaw sees me sitting in a hotel lounge drinking with a tall, attractive gentleman!'

Alex sipped his drink thoughtfully, looking away from her eyes.

'There's something on your mind,' she said, and he flushed guiltily. She was always so direct.

'There is indeed.' He nodded. 'I've had an offer . . . from America, in fact. I sometimes feel that my work here is finishing since few men now need the kind of surgery I carry out. Now I've been asked to go to America to set up a special clinic where I could study bone diseases and also teach my methods of surgery to . . . ' His voice fell away as he stared at Geraldine.

She looked almost shattered by this news. The colour had drained from her face and her eyes had filled with tears.

'Oh no!' she whispered. 'No, Alex

. . . not all the way to America! I might never see you again!'

He hadn't realised it would mean so much to her. Surely her life was not so empty. She had her three children.

Eleanor was now twenty-two, Terence, twenty, and Nancy, eighteen. Nancy was so full of life that she kept the old house, Hillcrest, echoing with her music and laughter.

Geraldine was pulling herself together. 'How like me!' She laughed a trifle unsteadily. 'Always thinking about myself! It's a good job Grandfather Wyllie can't see me! It was just a surprise, that's all, Alex. We've worked together for so many years, and somehow I thought it would go on for many more.'

'Geraldine, I . . . I'm sorry,' Alex said awkwardly. 'I didn't realise you depended on me for . . . '

'Help with the trust,' she finished quickly. 'Oh, but I do, Alex, or I did. Now don't worry another minute. As soon as I get used to the idea, I'll make other plans. In fact, I expect you've already got new ideas worked out . . . for the trust, I mean. It's been quite an evening, what with one thing and another.' She looked at her new watch, smiling. 'In fact, we'd better be on our way before I cause further talk by staying out all night!' But Alex knew she was still upset.

'Don't wait,' Geraldine said when they reached the station and found that there were still ten minutes to spare.

But Alex remained with her whilst Geraldine chattered to fill up the awkwardness between them. She had a carriage to herself and she had lowered the window and was leaning out of it while he stood outside on the platform.

Suddenly her attention was caught by the figure of a young girl rushing along the platform, her hat in her hand and her long fair hair streaming about her narrow shoulders.

'Nancy!' Geraldine's voice rang out, and the girl stopped short, blushing as she began to walk towards the compartment.

'Hello, Mum,' she said awkwardly, then turned to smile at Alex.

He was pleased to see her, glad that Geraldine would have her younger daughter's company on the way home.

'In here,' Geraldine was saying, and Alex Kinloch helped Nancy into the carriage, where she slumped into a seat.

'No need to wait now,' Geraldine told Alex.

'No, of course. I'll . . . I'll telephone you, Geraldine. We still have a few things to discuss. Good-night, my dear.'

★ ★ ★

'Now, young lady,' Geraldine said severely, 'perhaps you'll tell me what you're doing here in Edinburgh, and what kept you so that you almost missed the last train.'

Nancy looked at her, then beyond her out of the window.

'Oh, look, Mum!' she cried. 'Uncle Richard is in a show at The Belvedere in London. Just look! There's a picture of him and his leading lady. Richard Ransome and Sylvia Hess in 'Blue Rain'. Isn't he handsome? I'm going to stop calling him uncle now. Richard will do. After all, he's one of your oldest friends.'

'Why don't you call him Mr Ransome?' Geraldine asked tartly. 'After all, you always give Alex Kinloch his proper name.'

'Yes, but he's old, Mummy.'

'He's exactly the same age as Richard Ransome.'

'But Richard is much more glamorous,' Nancy objected, leaning back in her seat as the train chugged away from the station. 'I mean, he's been married to a Hollywood film star, and divorced, whereas Mr Kinloch hasn't ever been married.'

'Richard was the innocent party,' Geraldine put in quickly.

'I know. That's what makes it so much more exciting. He's divorced, but he hasn't done anything wrong. It was his wife who went off with another man . . . It was in all the papers.'

'Where were you?' Geraldine asked more loudly.

Nancy swallowed. 'I've been to Edinburgh to audition as a vocalist with Nat Singleton and his Orchestra.'

'Nat Singleton?' Geraldine stared at her daughter, who was refusing to wilt under her mother's baleful gaze.

Nancy was the musical one of the family and Geraldine had seen to it that her talents had been allowed to develop. She was now an accomplished pianist and her voice had been trained to sing the lovely Scottish ballads which her grandparents loved.

'It's out of the question! You must put this out of your mind, Nancy.'

Nancy's small face took on its stubborn look.

'I can't put it out of my mind, Mummy,' she said. 'You see, I've got the job. I have to go to London on Saturday, and start singing with Nat Singleton almost at once. Oh, Mummy, we might even be broadcasting sometimes. I'm so excited. You know, some of the other girls were doing snap numbers, but I tried out that new song, 'Those Foolish Things' and they loved it. They said I was hired straightaway. Oh, Mummy, you must let me go, you simply must.'

Geraldine's head was aching. It was all too much for one evening.

'I don't want to hear any more. Nancy!' she cried, her nerves ragged. 'I don't want to talk about it tonight.'

'OK, Mum,' Nancy agreed.

'And you must be here for your grandmother's birthday party. It's bad enough having Terry away at the moment.'

'That's on Thursday. Of course I'll be here.'

'We'll talk about it later,' Geraldine repeated firmly.

Walking home from the station they met Eleanor. She was in her uniform as Guide Mistress, which Geraldine felt did little for her looks. She was a pretty girl but, in her mother's opinion, she didn't make the most of herself.

'You're late home, Eleanor,' she remarked.

'I know, Mummy. I've been making the final arrangements for Saturday.'

'Saturday?'

'Oh, Mummy, you can't have forgotten!' Eleanor looked at her almost reproachfully. 'I'm taking the guides on a coach trip to Ayr. A few days by the sea. Some of them would never see the seaside otherwise. They look forward to it for weeks and weeks.'

'Of course . . . yes, I remember,' Geraldine said hastily and a trifle guiltily. Eleanor did a great deal of work among the children of Fairlaw. She had qualified as a teacher and was now teaching at Fairlaw Primary School, but whereas the other teachers seemed to shut off their work when they went home, Eleanor was inclined to live with it constantly. She gave too much of herself to other people, thought Geraldine fondly, as she felt her daughter's hand slipping into her own.

* * *

Breakfast was late the following morning. It was the first week of the summer holidays and Eleanor was not obliged to leave so early for school. Geraldine lay a little longer than usual in bed, listening to the faint sounds made by the housekeeper, Jenny Muir, as she lit the fire in the morning-room. Except in very hot weather, Mrs Wyllie always liked a fire on in the house.

Jenny Muir had been a young girl when Geraldine first came to Fairlaw. She had helped to bring up the children, and had often been a stalwart when Geraldine felt she could not stand living in Hillcrest one more minute.

When she and Laurence had first married, it had not been with the approval of Laurence's father, Stephen Wyllie. They had met when Laurence was sent to a London solicitors for a course in English law, and their wedding had been hastened because she and Laurence were both on active service during the Great War. Their love had been a burning passion made even more poignant because of the dangers they were facing.

Laurence was invalided out of the Army, having been wounded in France, Geraldine already having given up her ambulance work to make a home in London for them and their children, Eleanor and Terry. Nancy had been born just before the end of the war, in 1918.

It had not been easy to pull up her roots in London, thought Geraldine, as she rose and began to dress in a navy gaberdine skirt with a pink and white candy-striped blouse. Laurence's health had become poor in London and his father needed him in their solicitor's firm at Fairlaw. For a time she had been happy here, despite her father-in-law's disapproval of a daughter-in-law who had served a prison sentence for her suffragette activities.

Laurence had encouraged her to go to London often to see her own parents and Miss Margaret Temple, a greatly-loved friend of theirs. Sometimes, too, she had met Richard Ransome, whom she had known since childhood, and who had made his career on the stage.

When Geraldine went downstairs, she found Stephen Wyllie and his wife already in the morning-room, his arm round his wife's waist as she leaned heavily on her stick.

'You should have stayed in bed for breakfast,' Geraldine scolded, hurrying to settle her at the table, while Mr Wyllie lowered himself into a chair and picked up his newspaper.

A few moments later they were joined by Eleanor and when they had started breakfast Nancy hurried in rather furtively and took her place at the table.

'This man, Hitler, seems to be doing well for Germany,' Mr Wyllie pronounced when Jenny had removed his empty porridge plate and placed bacon and eggs in front of him.

'I think he's dangerous,' Geraldine argued.

'Dangerous? In what way? He's pulling his country together and giving them a bit of pride in themselves. What's so dangerous about that?'

'He's a dictator, Father, that's what. I like a prime minister who can be voted out at the next election if he doesn't mind his P's and Q's. Hitler is casting covetous eyes on the rest of Europe.'

'Nonsense, Geraldine. He wouldn't dare. Just listen to this.' He began to read from the paper, but was interrupted by Mrs Wyllie before he got very far.

'Is that your new watch, dear?' she asked mildly, and Geraldine turned to show the watch to her mother-in-law, politics forgotten for the moment.

The postman arrived with a number of early birthday cards for Mrs Wyllie. She had already received one from her daughter, Susan, who had been living on a mission station in Rhodesia for a number of years.

'Most of the mail is for you, Mother.'

Geraldine smiled. 'One from New Zealand, I see.'

'Open it first, Granny,' Nancy urged. 'I bet it's from Aunt Agnes and Uncle John, and my cousin, Anne. I bet she's spoiled to death by now. Aunt Agnes used to give her everything.'

'Oh, Nancy!' Eleanor said. 'She was always such a pretty baby. We all spoiled her.'

Mrs Wyllie's eyes misted as she looked at the lovely card from her younger daughter, Agnes. There was a long letter enclosed in the card and a note scribbled on the back that there was a present on the way.

She missed Agnes very much, as well as her son-in-law John and her youngest granddaughter, Anne. Yet many times she gave silent thanks that Agnes was living such a good life in New Zealand where John Howard was headmaster of a fine boys' school.

'Nothing yet from Aunt Margaret Temple in London,' Nancy remarked, betraying to her mother that her thoughts were not far away from the capital.

'Don't go out before I've had a chance to talk to you, Nancy,' Geraldine said quietly. 'I want a word after breakfast.'

'OK. Mummy,' Nancy sighed.

'There should be heaps of cards tomorrow as well,' Eleanor said, placing them along the mantelpiece. 'We haven't had one yet from Terry in Paris, or from the ladies of the Red Cross, or — '

'Can you give Jenny a hand, dear?' her mother interrupted. 'I want to talk to Nancy.'

'Of course,' Eleanor said readily, though she looked curiously at her younger sister. She recognised her mother's tone of voice, and wondered what Nancy had done now.

'We'll go through to the lounge,' Geraldine said to Nancy.

Nancy's mouth took on a mulish look and she glanced at Eleanor and her grandparents.

'I don't mind if we talk about it here, Mummy,' she said, her eyes very wide though her hands clutched her handkerchief nervously. 'I don't mind everyone knowing about my new job. After all, I have to leave on Saturday.'

* ★ ★ ★ *

Old Mr Wyllie laid his newspaper aside. 'What's all this, Nancy? Where are you going on Saturday?'

'I . . . I've got a marvellous new job . . . in London,' Nancy told him, her eyes beginning to shine with excitement. 'I'm going to sing with a wonderful big orchestra at a very grand hotel in London — and, Grandfather, just imagine, I could be on the radio.'

Constance Wyllie had laid aside her letter and was staring fixedly at Nancy, then her eyes went to Geraldine.

'It has not been decided yet, Nancy, whether or not you're going to be allowed to consider this job,' Geraldine began.

'Which band have you been offered a job with?' Eleanor asked.

'Nat Singleton's,' Nancy said, and they were silent for a moment. Even the grandparents had heard of Nat Singleton.

Geraldine felt torn in two. If only Nancy was a year or two older!

'They pay well,' Nancy said, naming her salary and again there was silence. It was almost three times Eleanor's salary, and as much as Stephen Wyllie had paid for a young qualified man before he sold the practice.

'That's ridiculous!' he cried. 'It's far too much for a girl of your age.'

'They wouldn't pay it if I wasn't worth it,' Nancy insisted. 'I want to go on Saturday. I'll ring up Aunt Margaret Temple and see if I can stay with her.'

'It's that Richard Ransome who's influencing you,' Stephen Wyllie said, glaring at Geraldine. 'I always said he would be a bad influence on the children!'

Geraldine said nothing. There was no

doubt that both Nancy and Terry idolised Richard. Richard had gathered a number of young theatrical people round him and was giving them a fine training for the stage. A party of them had gone to France for further study and Terry had pleaded with her to allow him to join the party even though he had no personal ambitions to go on the stage. He was more interested in politics. He wanted to travel on the continent and this was his chance.

'The man has been through the divorce courts,' was Mr Wyllie's parting shot.

'He was the innocent party,' Nancy defended. 'And I don't care what anyone says — I am going!'

★　★　★

The following morning Geraldine was up early, knowing that she had a busy day ahead of her before the party for Mrs Wyllie's seventieth birthday that evening. She had spent a restless night, trying to decide whether or not she should consent to Nancy going to London.

But her thoughts also dwelt on Alex Kinloch, who would be coming to the birthday party. Until his shock announcement that he was leaving, Geraldine hadn't realised how much she had come to like him, as well as respect him. All her love had been showered on Laurence, and since his death she had not as much as considered a relationship with another man. Now she must welcome Alex as though nothing had happened. She must not embarrass him further.

Old Mrs Wyllie spent most of the day in bed, but she was energetic and full of excitement when Geraldine and Jenny Muir helped her to get ready for her birthday party.

Geraldine stood beside her mother-in-law as they welcomed all their guests and she smiled warmly when Alex Kinloch walked in and brought sincere congratulations to old Mrs Wyllie, together with a gift of delicate perfume.

'Lovely to see you, Alex,' she said, her eyes meeting his clearly.

'Thank you for the invitation,' he said.

Later Mr Wyllie helped his wife to blow out her candles.

After the supper had been cleared away, Nancy was asked to sing for the guests, and she rose gracefully and walked to the piano.

Geraldine's eyes misted as she listened to the beauty and purity of her daughter's singing. Nancy really had a wonderful talent.

A hand touched her arm and she turned to see Jenny Muir looking at her anxiously, and gesticulating towards the hall.

'What's the matter, Jenny?' she asked, after she had slipped out and closed the door of the drawing-room.

'A young lady has arrived and wants to talk to you,' Jenny told her. 'She's a foreign lady. I've put her in the morning-room.'

'A foreign lady . . . wanting to see me?' Geraldine repeated, then hurried to the morning-room. A tall, young woman, wearing a black beret over her short, dark hair rose to her feet. The girl's face was very white, and her large eyes were made to look even bigger by the application of mascara and eye shadow. The make-up, however, failed to hide the fatigue on her face and she looked at Geraldine apprehensively.

'Can I help you?' Geraldine asked. 'Did you wish to see me?'

'I . . . I am disturbing you,' the girl said, backing away a little. 'There is a party . . .'

Geraldine's eyes narrowed as she saw apprehension growing in the girl. 'Never mind the party,' she said quickly. 'Who are you? Why do you wish to see me?'

'I . . . I am Maria Fischer,' the girl said huskily. 'I am a friend of Terence — Terence Wyllie.'

'Where is Terry? Why didn't he write to say you were coming?'

Suddenly, the girl's face seemed to crumple and she sat down on one of the chairs and began to sob.

'He . . . he cannot. He is caught,' she said thickly.

'Caught? Caught where?'

'He is in Germany — Berlin. He was helping me to get to France, but he is being questioned . . . by the Nazis!'

Geraldine's heart was hammering loudly. The girl was weeping helplessly, the mascara making black rivulets down her face.

Geraldine was lost for words. What was Terry doing in Berlin? He should be in Paris. Swiftly she poured a small tot of brandy and gave it to the girl who drank a little, then coughed.

After a moment the hot spirit revived her, and she began to speak so fast that Geraldine could make little of what she was saying. Maria Fischer had met Terry at an apartment house in Berlin, mainly used by theatrical people. He was there with the other young English people. They had become friends.

'I had to get away,' Maria was saying. 'I speak too freely, you see. I say my views, and they do not like it, so Terry promises help for me to leave. But he does not get away . . . '

Vaguely, Geraldine heard the sound of laughter and good wishes as the guests left, then the door of the morning-room opened and the rest of the family were all gathering round.

Maria Fischer looked like a trapped animal as she faced Terry's family and if Geraldine had not been so concerned for her son, her heart would have gone out to the girl.

But now she only had one thought in mind.

'Richard,' she said. 'Richard Ransome.' He must know something about this. After all, he had organised the trip to Paris.

Dear Richard . . .

Geraldine was trembling as she dialled the number of Richard Ransome's flat. Her frustration grew as the rings went unanswered. Eventually, she hung up.

A glance at the clock showed that he might possibly still be at the Belvedere Hotel, eating dinner, but when Geraldine rang, the man she spoke to was most evasive.

'I understand Mr Ransome is with a party of friends, madam,' the man told her smoothly, 'though, of course, we will try to contact him for you.'

'Very well, I shall telephone in ten minutes.' Geraldine was saying, then the rest of the family heard the receiver being banged into place.

'They're going to enquire if he is still in the hotel,' she told them. 'A few members of the party have gone on somewhere else. He could be with them. Nobody seems to know. I think they're being very discreet, but I'm in no mood for that.' Her gaze rested on old Mrs Wylie.

'I think you ought to go to bed, darling,' she told her gently. 'You look very tired. Don't worry, I'll tell you as soon as I know what's happening.'

'I'll help you, Gran.' Eleanor offered.

Geraldine couldn't keep still, and paced the floor in front of the fire. 'I'll try the flat again, then the hotel. I must do something.'

But again, her efforts were fruitless and, finally, she returned to the morning-room where Maria had been given a hot drink and a sandwich. The girl looked very tired.

'We'll have to go to London,' Geraldine declared. 'Miss Fischer — Maria — you'll have to come with me . . . '

Eleanor had returned to the morning-room and now she hurried over to the fireside. 'I don't think Gran's very well,' she said.

'You two girls can look after her,' Geraldine said. 'I must go to London to see Richard, and I'll take Maria with me. I'll arrange to go first thing in the morning.'

'Oh dear.' Eleanor was clearly upset. 'Oh, Mummy! What about the guides?'

'Terry is in grave trouble,' her mother said flatly. 'Nothing else matters but that. Of course, I realise your difficulties with the guides, dear.'

'I just can't let them down, but Gran can't be left,' Eleanor said distractedly.

'Nancy,' Geraldine said. 'You can cope, can't you, darling? You're a competent girl. You can cope very well with Gran.'

'Yes, but, Mummy, have you forgotten? I've got that marvellous job with Nat Singleton and I have to go on Saturday.'

Nancy's face had gone very white as she stared at her mother.

'My one big chance,' she whispered, almost to herself. 'I'll never get another.' She looked at her mother who was nervously pulling at the lace on her handkerchief. It showed all too clearly how upset she was and suddenly her fear communicated itself to Nancy.

Only Terry mattered, nothing else. She glanced at Eleanor.

'I'll stay,' she said huskily. 'You can't let the guides down, and Gran can't be left. I'll stay.'

Next morning Geraldine was awake before the alarm rang more than twice. She leaped out of bed, her head aching and her eyes smarting through lack of sleep, but a quick dash of cold water over her face made her feel better. She went to waken Maria.

'Time to get up,' she said urgently. 'I'm booking seats on the London train.'

The girl's dark eyes flew open and she stared at her, stark with fear. Then she relaxed and threw back the bedclothes.

Geraldine had little time to spare for her family as she packed an overnight bag, then quickly gave Nancy a hurried list of instructions.

'I'll be at Aunt Margaret Temple's
. . . I'd better telephone her . . . but I
shall see Richard Ransome as soon as
possible. Manage as best you can,
Nancy.'

Nancy was more subdued than her
mother had ever seen her.

'Come on, Maria, time to go,' Geraldine said briskly. 'I don't want to miss
the express. The next train is a stopper.'

It was late afternoon when they
reached Mountjoy Terrace near
Regent's Park where Aunt Margaret
had lived for years. Now in her
seventies, Margaret Temple was still an
active woman, even if she did not
possess the boundless energy which
had once been hers.

One look at Geraldine, however,
made Aunt Margaret's eyes widen with
concern and she took the younger
woman into her arms.

Maria stood behind her, looking
frightened and tired, and Aunt Margaret shepherded both of them into her

cosy sitting-room.

'Now, what's all this about?' she asked.

Geraldine dried the tears that had spilled down her cheeks. There was no time for such weakness. There was too much to do, and she swiftly repeated Maria's story of Terry's arrest in Berlin.

'Oh dear, that's very worrying.' The old lady took Geraldine's hand, unable to hide her own anxiety. 'But if he went to Paris with those young people, what was he then doing in Berlin?'

'That's what I want to know. What's the time, Aunt Margaret? I must see Richard Ransome.'

'But I've got a meal all ready for you!'

'I . . . I'm not hungry.' Geraldine's voice was strained.

'I've listened to that remark too often in the past. What time are you seeing Richard?'

'He ought to be at the theatre in about an hour's time to get ready for the evening's performance. Rehearsal will be past.'

'Enough time to eat a little.'

Neither Geraldine nor Maria had much appetite and Aunt Margaret did not press them as she began to realise how worried Geraldine must be.

'You will both stay here until this thing is resolved,' she said firmly to Geraldine. 'I'll be waiting up for you whatever time you get home.'

'Thank you, Aunt Margaret,' Geraldine whispered huskily, grateful for the comfort of the older woman. Then she called a taxi.

⋆   ⋆   ⋆

The doorman at the Belvedere Theatre recognised Geraldine. She had been coming to see Richard Ransome's shows for a great many years, sometimes by herself, then later with her children. He looked curiously at the girl who came with her, but he had no hesitation in admitting them to wait in Richard's dressing-room.

'He can arrive at any time, ma'am,'

the doorman informed her. 'Then, again, he could be a good hour yet. Sometimes he stays on after rehearsals. You never know where you are with Mr Ransome.'

Geraldine nodded her agreement. Richard was unpredictable, but sooner or later he would have to get ready for his show. She prowled up and down the floor of the dressing-room like a caged animal until the dressing-room door was thrust open and Richard Ransome strode in. He was very tall and handsome, his hair only lightly touched with grey, and his body still lean and athletic.

Richard stopped abruptly when he saw his visitors. Then his face lit up with pleasure.

'Geraldine!' he cried. 'What a lovely surprise! I'd no idea . . . '

'Where's Terry, Richard?' she demanded.

Richard paused, then grasped one of her hands, a frown gathering between his brows. He looked at Maria, then back to Geraldine.

'Terry . . . ?' she repeated. 'You've got to tell me what's happened. I allowed him to go with your party of young protégés to Paris because you were in charge of the group . . . '

'But isn't he back home with you?' Richard broke in. 'All the others are back here from Paris. They've been back in London for some weeks.'

Geraldine stared at him disconcertedly. 'Why did he go on to Berlin?' she asked. 'This young lady is Maria Fischer, who met Terry in Berlin. They were living in the same boarding house, mainly used by theatrical people, as I understand.'

Richard was shaking his head in bewilderment. 'I don't understand this at all,' he said. 'I thought he was back in Fairlaw.'

'He came to Berlin with friends,' Maria explained. 'There was a girl called Amanda Morris and a young man, James Corviso.'

'They were with the group,' Richard agreed. 'They're to be married.'

35

'That is so.' Maria nodded. 'They were in Berlin and they move on, but Terry stays.' The tears began to well in her eyes. 'He tried to help me, and . . . and now he is caught.'

'You've got to tell me what to do,' Geraldine said distractedly.

'All right,' Richard said soothingly. 'We'll sort this out, never fear. First of all, my understudy will have to do this show. I'll arrange that. Then I must make a few telephone calls. Wait here. I'll have coffee sent in, and you can tell me all about it from the beginning to end, every single little detail.'

It seemed hours before Richard came back, though there was purpose in his step and brisk efficiency in his manner.

'I haven't a lot of time, Geraldine,' he said, 'but I've made arrangements to travel to Berlin. I have to catch the boat train to Paris this evening. You'd better go back to Margaret Temple's — '

'I'm coming with you,' she said flatly. 'I'll take Maria back to Aunt Margaret's and pick up my overnight bag. Thank goodness I brought all the papers I might need — just in case of emergency. I'll meet you at the station, Richard. Is it the ten o'clock?'

He nodded. 'All right, I'll be waiting for you,' he said. 'Don't worry, I shan't let anything very terrible happen to Terry.'

Geraldine said nothing as she hurried from the theatre. In her book something very terrible already had happened to her son.

* * *

The night ferry train left Victoria Station at ten o'clock and was due to arrive in Paris the following morning. Geraldine had travelled on this train on other occasions, but she was in no mood to enjoy the journey. She couldn't face breakfast next morning so Richard just ordered coffee.

'Whatever possessed Terry?' Geraldine said for the tenth time. 'Why should he go on to Berlin?'

'He's waiting to go for army officer training, isn't he?' Richard asked. 'I know how much he admired his father for being an army officer.'

Geraldine nodded. Terry hated the law, but was passionately interested in military affairs.

'It must have been a great temptation, Geraldine,' Richard reasoned. 'He would want to see what's happening in Germany first hand, not merely by reading it up in the papers.'

'But he must know that the regime in Germany must be treated with great care. Oh, Richard!'

They had several hours to wait at the Gare du Nord in Paris while Richard tried to get them good accommodation on the train, but finally he came to tell her that they could take the Nord Express and change at Cologne.

They finally steamed into Berlin and Richard hurried her towards the exits. Then, suddenly, a tall man with a brown weather-beaten face began to move forward. He wore a dark blue uniform with an impressive peaked cap, and Geraldine could see that he had picked them out of the crowd and was walking towards them with purpose.

A moment later Richard had turned and the man's arms were suddenly outstretched, his face wreathed in smiles as they welcomed one another with great, bearlike hugs.

'Geraldine, this is my old friend, Karl Weiss,' Richard said happily. 'We met in Switzerland years ago when I was learning to ski. Karl is a great champion.'

'Alas, no longer, my friend,' Karl said, pumping Geraldine's hand. 'Now I must teach the young ones, but I have been appointed warden of a fine new sports centre here in Berlin. I look very good, no?'

'Absolutely splendid,' Richard agreed.

'I was so happy you made the telephone call,' Karl was saying. 'I have booked two rooms as you requested, Richard, at the Westerburg Hotel. Very quiet. Very nice. I have a car waiting.'

As the car swung out into the busy traffic of the Berlin streets, Richard began to explain their errand.

'Mrs Wyllie's son, Terence, appears to have involved himself in a little bit of trouble, Karl,' he said quietly.

'What sort of trouble, my friend?' Karl asked.

Richard began to explain the circumstances.

'We don't know the full facts, but we do know that he met a young lady here . . . '

'Ah, the young lady,' Karl Weiss broke in, beaming again. 'For a young man, there is always the young lady. You want to know if she is just right for your son, Frau Wyllie?'

'Not that, Karl,' Richard said quickly. 'The young lady appears to have been indiscreet and has talked against certain aspects of the Nazi policies, or perhaps even members of the Nazi authorities. She felt it would be wise to leave Germany and it appears Terence helped her to obtain false papers. The young lady is now in England, but Terence is being held here for questioning by the authorities. We've come here to obtain his release.'

Karl Weiss had gone very quiet. 'I cannot help you, Richard,' he said in a low voice, after he had installed them in the hotel. 'I must leave you now because I am very busy, you understand. I have no influence, I regret.'

'But you must know somebody — '

'I am sorry.' Karl shook Richard's hand formally, and glancing at Geraldine made to leave. Then he turned to Richard again.

'Listen carefully, my friend. I will give you the name and telephone number of someone who can help, but you must not mention my name. You must not tell anyone at all that I helped you — it would not be good for me. You understand? Listen carefully because I can write nothing down.'

Richard repeated the name and telephone number twice over, and the other man nodded, satisfied.

'I hope things go well for you,' he said.

'Goodbye, Karl, and thank you,' Richard said gratefully.

The man bowed briefly and made his way out of the hotel.

'He was afraid, wasn't he?' said Geraldine, almost in a whisper.

'More terrified, I'd say.'

'Then the quicker we do something, the better,' Geraldine said nervously.

'We'll have to leave it until tomorrow,' said Richard. 'It's too late to do anything this evening.'

★   ★   ★

Geraldine was up early the following morning as the noisy sounds of Berlin seemed to beat upon her closed windows. She leaped out of bed and looked down on the street below. Everyone was in a hurry, many on bicycles, weaving their way in and out amongst the traffic. Some of the cars carried men in the now-familiar uniform of the Nazi stormtrooper, and some young people walked along in a crowd, their behaviour rowdy and arrogant, whilst older people quickly made way for anyone in authority.

Geraldine had arranged to meet Richard downstairs in the dining-room, and she found him waiting for her, looking spruce and elegant in his dark suit and white shirt.

'What are you going to do, Richard?' she asked urgently.

'Patience, Geraldine. First we must eat. A quick breakfast and then I can start to use the telephone. Now, drink up your coffee.'

Geraldine drank her coffee then wandered into the lounge to wait for Richard. She picked up a discarded newspaper, but her German wasn't good enough to read it accurately.

Richard came back to tell her he had to go out for an hour or two, and advised her, rather hurriedly, to remain where she was.

'But, Richard!' she cried. 'I — '

'I'll be as quick as I can,' he

interrupted and was gone.

Geraldine watched the swing doors closing behind him, then she went slowly up to her room and collected her handbag. She could not sit still any longer. She had to get out.

A moment later she was walking out of the hotel into the streets of Berlin and trying to imagine that these were the very streets which Terry had walked along only a short time ago, perhaps with Maria Fischer beside him.

The noisy, rowdy atmosphere seemed to become much more acute here and with it Geraldine's fears multiplied. She saw pedestrians being jostled by swaggering uniformed men, and the pale look of strain on others. With a shiver of apprehension Geraldine turned and retraced her steps to the hotel. She hoped terribly that Richard would be back with some news of Terry.

But it was an hour later before Richard returned and by then Geraldine's nerves were so ragged that she rushed to meet and embrace him as soon as he appeared in the doorway.

'Oh, Richard, I'm so glad you're back,' she said breathlessly. 'What . . . what have you found out?'

'Not a great deal,' he replied. 'But I saw some people, people who can help us and now we must wait for a telephone call. We'll just have to be patient.'

'Patient!' she cried. 'How can we be patient when my son — ?'

He took her in his arms and held her close. 'Please,' he breathed into her hair. 'I know it's not easy, but there's nothing else we can do.' He managed to calm her down, but it seemed ages before he was called to the telephone. Geraldine waited nervously and sprang to her feet when he returned.

'Well?' she demanded.

'I have to go out again, Geraldine, but this time I'm hoping to get some positive results.'

'Oh, that's wonderful. Where are you going?'

'Don't ask too many questions. Trust

me.' He smiled at her reassuringly, opening his briefcase and checking his passport and wallet, and suddenly she began to understand.

'If there's money involved, Richard, you must let me pay. Terry is my responsibility.'

Richard snapped his briefcase shut, then he turned to her, a slight glint in his eyes.

'No, Geraldine, it's my responsibility. I was the one who sent Terry abroad in the first place. All this is my fault. Wait here for me, darling. I don't know how long this is going to take.'

It was the early evening before Richard arrived back at the hotel. But this time he was smiling.

'It's all right, Geraldine, you can relax now,' he told her gently. 'Our worries are over. Terry has just been driven to the airport and put on a plane for Paris. He's been deported. I have no doubt that he will be back in London before we are.'

Geraldine listened, but he had to tell

her again before she could take in what he was saying.

'No need to be afraid any more, Geraldine,' he told her, stroking her hair. 'It's all over now!'

'Oh, Richard.' Her voice was choked and muffled with tears. 'I shan't ever be able to thank you.'

'No need for thanks. I don't want any of that talk,' he told her brusquely. 'Now, darling, shall we check in here for another night and book on the early-morning train?'

'Oh no, I'd rather go now,' she said quickly. 'I'll ride on a cattle wagon if needs be.' She lowered her voice again. 'I hate this place. I just want to get away.'

'All right, I'll arrange it,' he said comfortingly. She gave a small sigh. It was wonderful to be able to leave things to Richard.

★　★　★

The only accommodation Richard could get on the night train was a small compartment that they would have to share. It was small and cramped, but the train was crowded and Geraldine knew they were lucky to have anything at all.

'Try to rest, Geraldine,' he said. 'It may be cold later. I have packed a sweater, though, so I won't need this jacket. It would cover you quite nicely if you need it.'

He had removed the jacket and turned to look at her so that their eyes met. Her heartbeats quickened.

Richard turned away, his mouth tightening a little. He knew Geraldine very well, and knew that she was grateful, but he did not want gratitude from her.

'Try to get some rest,' he told her tersely. 'It's going to be a long and tiring journey home.'

He heard her sigh as though she had been holding her breath, then she turned over and settled down to rest. But although she was very tired, Geraldine could not sleep. To her own secret shame, she felt disappointed that Richard had not wanted to take her in his arms, or even to kiss her good-night.

Back in London, Geraldine insisted that she should get a taxi, on her own, and return to Aunt Margaret's house in Mountjoy Terrace, but Richard insisted equally firmly that he would accompany her.

'I want to see young Terry in the flesh,' he said. 'I want to be absolutely sure that he really is back home, and is in good health.'

When they reached Aunt Margaret's house, the door was opened almost immediately and Terry stood there, grinning hugely, his arms outstretched to hug his mother.

'Oh, Terry!' She gasped. 'What a fright you gave us. I was beginning to think I might never see you again. Thank goodness Richard knew the right people, and how to go about getting you released. You owe your freedom to him.'

Richard was behind her and he, too,

hugged the boy and patted his shoulder. 'You didn't have any more trouble?' he asked.

'Not too much, beyond a few insults.'

'Whatever possessed you to go to Germany?' Geraldine demanded. 'You didn't even write to tell us about it!'

'It seemed such a golden opportunity,' he said, then turned appealingly to Richard. 'You know what I mean, Uncle Richard. One or two people were going on to Berlin and I wanted to see for myself how things were there, especially since I'll be joining the Army myself soon. I didn't really believe that they were clamping down on the Jews, and no-one was free to say what they wanted.

'We found quite nice theatrical accommodation with nice people, one of them a Nazi. I went out into the streets, sat in the bars and made friends with other young men, including Nazis.' He shook his head. 'No, not exactly friends with any Nazi. They are a breed on their own. Ask Maria.'

'Well, I shall want to know all about it later,' his mother warned him. 'So will Richard.'

Terry nodded. He had expected nothing less.

Suddenly the small house was full of laughter as Aunt Margaret appeared from the kitchen, along with Maria Fischer who was enveloped in one of Aunt Margaret's voluminous overalls.

'Tonight I cook a dish for you all,' she said happily, and poked Terry in the ribs. 'A German dish.'

'In that case, I shall have baked beans on toast,' Geraldine declared.

'And I must leave straight away for the Belvedere Theatre,' Richard put in. 'The show must go on,' he told her, grinning. 'Goodbye for now, Geraldine. I . . . I'll be in touch.'

She nodded gravely and saw him to the door. She had depended on him so much over the past few days and now she felt lonely without him, even though she was back with her family again.

'I can't believe we've both got away,' Terry was saying as he put an arm round Maria's shoulders, then turned to look at his mother. Geraldine paused as she went back into Aunt Margaret's sitting-room. Terry was so happy and relieved to be home, but there was more than that in his glowing looks.

He was in love with Maria Fischer, thought Geraldine. He and this German girl, whose upbringing and background were so different from his own, were in love with one another.

A Second Chance

As soon as she had a chance, Geraldine telephoned Fairlaw. Terry had called his grandparents when he had reached Aunt Margaret's and they had been overjoyed that he was safe.

'How is everyone?' Geraldine asked Nancy, who had answered the telephone. 'Is Gran OK?'

'Oh yes, she was fine after a rest,' Nancy told her. 'She overdid it a little, at the party, what with all the excitement and everything.'

'And Eleanor?'

'Her long weekend at Ayr seems to have been quite a success. She keeps talking about it and about the people she met . . . '

'And you, Nancy? Have you picked up a cold?'

'Oh no, Mummy!' The muffled note

in Nancy's voice sounded even more clearly.

'Did you ring up Nat Singleton's secretary? When are you coming to London now, darling?' Geraldine asked.

'I'm not,' ' Nancy said flatly. 'I . . . I lost the job, Mummy.' Her young voice was steady, but Geraldine almost recoiled at the unfamiliar harsh note in it.

'You . . . you lost the job?' she repeated.

'Of course I did. Didn't you think I would, Mummy? You must have known that for every girl like me, there are dozens just as good waiting to leap into my shoes. I tried to explain to . . . to the secretary and the manager, but they weren't in the least interested. In a job like this, one never never lets people down.'

Nancy's sobs went right to Geraldine's heart as she tried to find the right words to comfort her daughter. Nancy had lost her big chance, and it was Geraldine herself who had insisted that

Nancy stay at home while she went to Germany. Slowly she made her way to the dining-room, where the others had already begun their meal.

'It was Karl who reported us,' Maria was saying. 'You know that, do you not, Terry?'

'He looked so harmless at the boarding house.' Terry shook his head.

'We used to laugh at the Nazis,' Maria went on. 'No longer. They can be brutal, cruel. I was so afraid that they would beat you, Terry. Had you been German, they would have beaten you.'

'Are you tired, dear?' Aunt Margaret asked, looking with concern at Geraldine's face after they finished their meal and returned to the sitting-room.

Geraldine was pale, but her eyes were bright.

'I am tired,' she agreed. 'I'm also very angry. What time is it?' she asked, turning to look at the clock. 'Yes, I think I might just have time . . . '

'For what?'

'To go to see Nat Singleton — at the

Marchand Hotel. I'll have a bath and change my clothes. I want to go now and settle this matter.'

Geraldine disappeared up to her room and when she returned there was little sign of fatigue on her face. She wore a beautiful dark red silk suit, and the lovely pearl and diamond earrings which had been one of Laurence's last gifts to her.

Aunt Margaret's eyes widened in surprise.

'You look very smart, dear!'

'Thank you. I was hoping you would say that. I don't intend to allow anyone to prevent me from seeing Mr Singleton.'

★ ★ ★

'Mr Singleton's orchestra is playing at the moment, madam,' was the disinterested greeting she received.

'There is an interval, isn't there?' said Geraldine, and the receptionist quailed under her determined glare.

'Yes, of course. I'll show you where you can wait, madam.'

The room was small but comfortable, though it seemed a long time before the door opened and Nat Singleton walked in, wiping his face wearily with a white handkerchief. He looked startled when he saw Geraldine waiting for him.

'Who are you? he said as she rose to her feet.

'This won't take long, Mr Singleton,' she replied clearly. 'I'm Geraldine Wyllie. Nancy's mother.'

'What can I do for you?'

'She has been so very disappointed, Mr Singleton, because you no longer want her.'

'As I remember it, she didn't keep her appointment with us. We can't afford unreliable girls, Mrs Wyllie.'

'There were special circumstances.' Mr Singleton,' said Geraldine. 'I'd better explain what they are . . . '

'Well, if you must — but I'm very tired.'

She did so as clearly as possible.

'Is that it?' he said finally.

She nodded and sat down again. 'I apologise,' she said, her cheeks beginning to glow with colour. 'I can see I'm wasting my time. I'm blaming you when it's not really your responsibility. I . . . I was impulsive. My daughter is so upset!'

Geraldine felt close to tears and hurriedly she rose to her feet.

'I'll check with my secretary, but I don't think any auditions have yet been held,' he told her. 'I could give Nancy a second chance, but she would have to understand that reliability is everything.'

'Oh, I'm sure Nancy understands that, Mr Singleton. She's an intelligent girl, and very talented. But I'm sure you know that.'

'Nancy is lucky,' said Nat Singleton, his eyes gleaming with humour. 'Not all girls have such splendid champions. If she can be here in, say, two days for rehearsals with the orchestra, I can use her next Saturday evening.'

'Mr Singleton, I don't know how to thank you.'

'Just see to it that Nancy doesn't let me down,' he said, and looked at his watch. 'Time I was on duty again. Good-night, Mrs Wyllie. Nice to have met you.'

★   ★   ★

Back at Mountjoy Terrace, fatigue took hold of her again and she was happy to allow Aunt Margaret to make a fuss of her.

'We must leave for Fairlaw in the morning,' she told Terry and Maria. 'I have to see Nancy. You'd better have everything packed ready to go in the morning.'

'It's been such a short visit,' said Aunt Margaret.

'And you've been wonderful, as always,' said Geraldine. 'Can you put Nancy up for a week or two until she finds her feet?'

'You know I can,' said Aunt Margaret. 'I'm delighted that it's going to be all right for her after all.'

Maria Fischer was looking at them with uncertainty.

'Shall . . . shall I stay in London?' she asked. 'Perhaps I could get a job here.'

'Oh no, I can't leave you here, Maria.' Terry said quickly. 'You'll have to come back home with Mother and me.'

Eleanor was the first to spot their arrival. She was at the gate, waving goodbye to a handsome if carelessly-dressed young man.

'Matt Pollock!' Terry exclaimed, looking at his mother. 'What's he doing at Hillcrest?'

'I don't know,' said Geraldine, 'but I've no doubt Eleanor can tell us.' She looked after the young man who was walking away.

Matt Pollock's reputation wasn't of the best in Fairlaw.

Eleanor looked quite taken aback for the moment when she saw her mother, Terry and Maria walking home from the station. Then she gave a cry of delight and ran towards them.

'Oh, Terry, I'm so glad to see you!' she cried.

'And you don't know how glad I am to see you, Eleanor,' he replied, laughing.

'Where's Nancy?' Geraldine asked, when Eleanor linked arms with her as they walked up the drive.

'She's gone to the pictures. First house. Gary Cooper in 'Mr Deeds Goes To Town'. She was terribly depressed, but one of her friends wanted her to go, so I talked her into it to cheer her up.'

It was a happy evening as they all sat round the fire and Terry told them about his experience in Germany, then demanded to hear what had been happening at home.

Later Geraldine found an opportunity to ask Eleanor about Matt Pollock. 'You came to the gate with him,' she said, 'so I presume he wasn't a casual caller.'

'He came to pick up some extra

books and drawing materials for his young sister — Cathy,' Eleanor replied, a bright sparkle in her eyes as she looked at her mother. 'As a matter of fact Matt has called round once or twice. At my invitation. Cathy's one of my guides, She's also in my class at school. She wouldn't have been in the guides if I hadn't helped her to get the uniform and . . . and the extra things she needed for the weekend in Ayr.' She paused breathlessly before rushing on.

'It was Matt who came with her to collect them. He's really a very nice young man, Mummy, only he hasn't had much of a chance in life. None of the Pollocks have. The parents don't look after them properly. Sarah Pollock is very happy-to-lucky . . . '

'I know what Mrs Pollock is like,' said Geraldine quietly. 'I've done my best for them all, especially when the children were small. I don't think you ought to . . . to be associating with Matt, however.'

'Mummy, I — '

Suddenly there was the sound of Nancy's voice in the hall and Eleanor paused as her young sister burst into the room.

'Oh, Mummy, you're back!' she cried. 'And Terry! Oh, I'm so glad you're all home.'

Geraldine hugged her younger daughter close.

'If I'd known you were coming I wouldn't have gone to the pictures,' Nancy said. 'But . . . but I had to do something to get out of the house for a little while. Oh, Mummy, it's been awful . . .

'It's the early train for you in the morning,' her mother announced. 'Nat Singleton is expecting you tomorrow afternoon for rehearsal. I saw him for you. It's all fixed.'

'You . . . you mean I can still go to London?'

'I mean you can still go to London,' Geraldine assured her.

'Oh, Mummy!' Nancy laughed and cried in turns, then she threw her arms around her mother's neck.

The old house settled down once more after Nancy had gone to London. Maria was quietly accepted by the family, though the atmosphere in the house changed subtly.

Newspaper headlines proclaimed the storm clouds gathering over Germany, and Geraldine became aware of the sideways glances and the sudden silences which greeted her and Maria as they went shopping together.

Beyond a brief note, Geraldine hadn't heard from Richard Ransome, but she was delighted to receive a telephone call from Alex Kinloch, inviting her out to dinner.

'I phoned once or twice, but you were away,' he told her.

'Oh, I'm sorry, Alex, but we had a problem. I'll tell you all about it when we meet. And I'm sure you must have some news for me, too!'

'I have and it's good news,' said Alex. 'I'm not now going to America.'

'Oh, I am glad,' Geraldine said warmly.

'I'll book dinner for us tomorrow night,' said Alex. 'I'm looking forward to seeing you, Geraldine.'

Geraldine took care over her appearance as she dressed for her dinner date. Green suited her and she wore a slim-fitting suit with a matching hat whose sweeping brim dipped over one eye.

Alex looked very tall and distinguished, his manner always slightly more stiff and correct than that of Richard Ransome, but tonight his eyes were bright with eagerness as he greeted her.

'It seems months since I've seen you instead of a few weeks,' he said. 'I know, of course, that you had to go to Germany.'

'Yes, I had little time for explanations, Alex,' said Geraldine apologetically, as they were shown their table.

After they had ordered she told Alex all about her trip to Berlin with Richard Ransome.

'It wasn't his fault that Terry decided to go on to Berlin from Paris,' she ended. 'Terry's waiting to go to Officers' Training shortly, and he wanted to see how things were in Germany at first hand. And then he met Maria and he came too closely involved for comfort!'

Alex studied her face intently, though there was a tiny crease between his eyes. And you travelled with Ransome across France and into Germany?'

'Certainly we did.' Geraldine's eyes were wide and clear. 'Richard and I are old friends.'

Alex nodded, then he applied himself to his sirloin steak. Geraldine just did not understand. She had her reputation to consider. Laurence had always allowed her plenty of freedom, but he had been a stalwart in her life, supporting and guiding her.

If any woman needed a man to care for her, and to guide and protect her then surely that woman was Geraldine. She tended to act first and think later. Even now she was giving a home to the German girl, Maria Fischer, and that could mean all sorts of problems these days.

'You've still got the girl with you?' he asked.

'Yes.' For a moment her eyes were troubled. 'She and Terry are ... are very good friends.'

'I see,' said Alex. Then he reached over and pressed her fingers and she felt warmed by his understanding. She didn't have to spell out her troubles to Alex.

Maria was a nice girl and had tried to get a job in Fairlaw, but the local people seemed unwilling to employ a German girl. She managed to earn pin-money by coaching students in German, but she still stuck out like a sore thumb in the community.

She used heavy make-up and the most ordinary dress took on a new look as soon as Maria dropped it over her head. Terry was head over heels in love with her. Already he was anxious that Maria should remain at Hillcrest after he went for Officers' Training. He didn't want to lose her, but Geraldine sensed that she found Fairlaw very quiet after Berlin.

'Would you care for a sweet?' Alex was asking.

'No, thank you, I've had sufficient,' said Geraldine as they went through to the lounge for coffee. 'This is lovely,' she said, relaxing more happily. 'So your plans were changed over America?'

'Yes.' Alex looked serious. 'I may be needed for similar work in Britain,' he said. 'I just hope it doesn't come to another war.'

She nodded, her face pale. It had all happened before, with Laurence. Surely it could not happen again, with Terry.

Alex looked at her silently. Geraldine was a beautiful woman, but there was something vulnerable about her. He cared about her a great deal. In fact, he loved her. But he would have to consider marriage very carefully. He had spent many years on his own and marriage would mean a great upheaval for him.

Geraldine was looking at her new watch. 'Oh dear, I'm afraid I'll have to run again, Alex. It's time for my train. I've had a lovely evening.'

'So have I,' Alex mumbled. He wanted to say so many things, but already she was on her feet. Swiftly he settled the account, then together they hurried to the station. What he really wanted to say would have to wait for another time.

★   ★   ★

For Nancy the time was passing in a haze of sheer delight. She could hardly believe that her life had suddenly become so exciting, as she travelled to the rehearsal rooms each day, then to the Marchand Hotel, where she had made her debut with Nat Singleton and his orchestra.

Flowers began to arrive for her, and invitations to night clubs and social occasions, but Miss Morris, Nat Singleton's secretary, had vetoed most of them. Nancy frowned a little. She wasn't exactly a child, and some of the invitations were very attractive.

Unknown to Miss Morris, she had accepted one or two, and had been escorted to a number of lavish parties by young men who appeared to be in great demand, and who treated her like royalty.

The rehearsal rooms were buzzing with talk when Nancy walked in and greeted the members of the orchestra with a happy smile. She was getting to know all of them very well, especially Jimmy Arnold, who played the clarinet and also sang with the orchestra. Jimmy almost grabbed her arm as she walked round the door.

'Broadcast next week,' he told her. 'Two numbers for you, one for me. We need extra rehearsals, though.'

Nancy's heart lurched, then raced furiously with excitement. She was going to broadcast to the nation.

Everyone listened in to Nat Singleton from the Marchand Hotel.

'Oh, Jimmy!' she breathed. 'I'll be so nervous!'

'Not you!' he said cheerfully. 'Besides, you've got someone waiting to see you. A reporter, I think . . . '

'A reporter!'

'Yes. He wants to do an article on you for the 'London Scene' magazine. He's over there.'

A young man with unruly brown curls was making his way towards her, along with a photographer.

'Nancy Wyllie?' he asked. 'I'm Jonathan Duke. I've just heard you're broadcasting next week and we want to do a write-up. Now, if we can take one or two photographs, then just ask a few questions.' They sat in a corner of the practice rooms and Nancy found herself answering all sorts of questions about her life, and her home background. Jonathan Duke was easy to talk to and his bright blue eyes swept over her with admiration. She thought he had a lovely smile.

'I expect there's a queue,' he said, after he had snapped his notebook shut.

'A queue?'

'To take you out.' He smiled that lovely smile. 'Don't be surprised if I join it one of these days.'

She laughed. 'You'd better write a good article then, Mr Duke.'

'Jonathan. Mr Duke never sounds quite right for me . . . ah . . . Miss Wyllie.'

'Nancy,' she said, laughing.

'Don't be surprised then if I'm hanging around this evening. Maybe I could see you home?'

'Maybe.'

But there was no sign of Jonathan Duke that evening and Nancy, for the first time since coming to London, felt rather disappointed. However, she put all that behind her as she gave Aunt Margaret the exciting news about her broadcast, then telephoned home to Fairlaw. It was Geraldine who answered the telephone, and her reaction was all that Nancy had hoped for.

'Broadcast! Oh, Nancy, that's wonderful, darling! What time?' Geraldine asked. 'I'll write it all down to be sure there's no mistake,' she added. 'I must go and tell the others!'

On the evening of the broadcast Geraldine arranged the whole family around the wireless in the drawing-room. Even old Mr and Mrs Wyllie were excited at the prospect.

The wireless was of the very latest design and the reception was excellent. Geraldine's heart raced as Nat Singleton introduced Nancy, whose two numbers were to be 'Those Foolish Things' and 'I'll Follow My Secret Heart.'

How rich and sweet Nancy's voice sounded, thought Geraldine, feeling the sudden rush of tears to her eyes. How wonderful that they could listen to Nancy from so many miles away.

She looked at her mother-in-law and saw that Constance Wyllie, too, was very moved by the broadcast and that

Stephen Wyllie was clearing his throat noisily. It was a proud moment for all of them.

That evening Terry seized his chance to talk to his mother on her own. He was due, shortly, to leave for his Officers' Training Unit in Edinburgh, and he came to Geraldine's bedroom.

'I . . . ah . . . wanted to talk to you, Mother,' he began. 'It's about Maria.'

'What about Maria?'

'I . . . we're in love, and I . . . well . . . I wanted to ask her to marry me before I go to training college. I think Maria would feel better about staying on here if it was all official. I'm taking her out on Saturday night, a sort of last fling before I have to go, and I want to ask her then.'

'Oh, Terry!' Geraldine bit her lip. 'You're very young, darling. Wouldn't it be better to wait for a year or two?'

'Because she's German? Would you say the same thing if she were a local girl?'

Geraldine couldn't answer. She liked

74

Maria, but although the girl was little older than Terry, it seemed that she was years older in experience. Terry couldn't marry just yet, but Maria . . . Geraldine moved uneasily . . . Maria was a passionate girl who might find it difficult to wait for Terry.

She stared at her son unhappily, wishing as she did so many times before, that he had a father to talk to.

'I thought I'd tell you first, Mum,' he said quietly. 'But that's how it's going to be.'

She nodded and he kissed her cheek, then he went out of the room, quietly closing the door.

'I Want To Talk To You'

A copy of 'London Scene' arrived by post on Tuesday morning and Geraldine leafed through it until she found the article written about her daughter by Jonathan Duke.

The rest of the family read it with pride and pleasure.

'What do you think of it, Gran?' Terry asked.

Old Mrs Wyllie clipped on her spectacles. 'I can hardly believe that it's Nancy,' she said, staring at the picture. 'I've looked at so many photographs like this. It's strange to think she belongs to us.'

'I know what you mean, darling,' said Geraldine smiling.

Later in the morning she found time to look through the rest of her London paper. Nancy had mentioned that there were rumours that the King, Edward

VIII, had become very friendly with an American lady, Mrs Wallis Simpson, but Geraldine couldn't believe there was anything in the rumours beyond the usual gossip.

She turned a page and suddenly, her heart leaping, she found herself looking at a large photograph of Richard Ransome. He was smiling into the lovely face of Eve Tarrant, his new leading lady.

Romance For Ransome? the caption asked. Was Eve Tarrant the woman he had been waiting for?

Slowly Geraldine sat back in her chair, feeling shaken. Somehow she had felt so close to Richard for so many years without thinking too deeply about her feelings for him. She had known him almost all her life and he had always been around when she needed him.

When he was in America they wrote and there had been the occasional phone call when he was in London. But it seemed to her that there would always be a strong bond between them. Now it shook her to realise that perhaps Richard did not see things that way.

Quickly Geraldine threw the paper aside and stood up. She was indulging in childish fancies. Richard was still a young, very attractive man and it was surely the most natural thing in the world for him to fall in love with his new leading lady. She cut out the photograph of Nancy, and the article by Jonathan Duke, then she pasted it into an album she had bought for the purpose. Then she dropped the rest of the paper in the incinerator. She mustn't dwell on Richard Ransome. She had her own life to live.

* * *

With the money she had received for coaching her students in German, Maria bought a very special dress for Saturday evening. It was a long dinner gown in slinky black satin, which managed to reveal a great deal of her lovely figure.

Geraldine wondered how she could wave Terry and Maria away for their dinner date without Stephen Wyllie setting eyes on the girl!

'Well, my dear, you look very smart,' said Geraldine.

Maria beamed happily and a few minutes later Terry appeared, also clad in his dinner jacket. How tall he was, and broad, thought Geraldine. Had Laurence looked so very young to his parents when he and Geraldine first married?

Perhaps she had looked as alien to them as Maria did to her; yet how they had loved one another, and how happy they had been!

'Don't wait up, Mum,' said Terry cheerfully.

Swiftly he escorted Maria out to the car, opening the door for her then running round to the driver's seat.

'You look sensational, darling,' he told her admiringly. 'Would it spoil your lipstick if I kissed you?'

'I put it on so carefully for you.' Maria laughed. 'So we spoil it later. First we eat!'

He had booked a table at a hotel a few miles out of Fairlaw on the Edinburgh road where, later, there would be dancing to a five-piece band and where Maria's sensational gown was only one of many. They were shown to their corner table and they enjoyed themselves, thoroughly studying the menu and trying out dishes which were new to Maria. She reached out and caught Terry's hand.

'I would be so happy if you were not going away,' she said sadly.

'None of that tonight,' he told her. 'Tonight we enjoy ourselves. You must know why I've brought you here, darling.'

'For fun.'

'Yes, and for something more serious, Maria. I can't marry yet for at least two years, but we could be engaged. I do want to marry you, my darling. I love you so much. Do say we can be engaged and we'll get married as soon as I've finished my training.'

Maria's eyes were like huge lamps in her face. 'Engaged?' she repeated. 'But, Terry, your family . . . they will not like it.'

'Of course they will. They love having you at Fairlaw.'

'I am German. I am different from them.'

'What does that matter? All that matters is that we love each other. If we're engaged then you'll be one of the family.'

She stared at him. 'You do this to make it easy for me.'

'I do this because I want you desperately,' said Terry. 'Surely you can see how much I'm in love with you.'

She was smiling. 'It is for me, too,' she agreed softly. 'We are in love. We are engaged.'

Terry exclaimed with delight so that a few amused glances were cast in their direction. Then he searched in his pocket and brought out a lovely ruby and diamond engagement ring.

'I chose a ruby because it's so like my Maria — warm and colourful and beautiful,' he murmured tenderly.

Maria held out her right hand, but Terry reached for her left and slipped the ring on to her third finger. He had already found out the size from one of her costume jewellery rings. Now it sparkled in the soft light of a wall lamp.

'It is beautiful,' she breathed. 'I am engaged.'

'And you love me?' He smiled tenderly as she admired the ring.

'I love you,' she said simply.

$\star \quad \star \quad \star$

With her second broadcast behind her, and publication of the article by Jonathan Duke, Nancy was becoming much more confident and every day was proving to be more exciting than the previous one. She was beginning to accept more invitations out and to

82

attend parties with crowds of young people.

She had met Jonathan Duke at several of these functions, and he had excitedly told her how he was writing articles on sporting personalities, like Fred Perry and Henry Cotton.

'Though I expect we'll all be digging up what we can on Mrs Simpson,' he told Nancy. 'There will be no room for anything else.'

'My mother doesn't believe there's anything between her and the King,' said Nancy.

'She probably doesn't believe there's a war coming either,' said Jonathan gloomily, 'but there is. Don't you think it's time you went home, young Wyllie? You'll ruin that nightingale voice of yours if you breathe in this smoky atmosphere much longer.'

'I've come with friends,' said Nancy.

'Playboys. Not your style. Get your wrap and I'll drop you off at your digs.'

'But it's early yet.'

'Not for a working girl.'

Nancy hardly knew why she obeyed him and later, as she let herself into Aunt Margaret's with her own key, she felt irritated that Jonathan Duke had taken her away from all the fun and glitter of the party. Who was he to dictate to her? He had treated her as though she were a child!

Yet . . . she liked him, Nancy decided, as she crawled into bed. He had impressed on her that work came first before amusement, and there was something nice and solid about Jonathan Duke.

Nancy phoned home regularly and often spoke to Maria. She was delighted to hear about her brother's engagement and pleased that Maria shared such an interest in the threatre with her.

'Some day I will get a part on the stage.' Maria sighed, as she talked to Nancy. 'I will be another Elizabeth Bergner.'

'Good luck then,' said Nancy. 'If I can help you, I will.'

A few evenings later she had changed

into a new ultra-smart evening gown in gold satin for yet another date. People were beginning to notice her, and she had to spend a lot of her earnings on clothes. But all the late nights began to take their toll.

On the second morning she was late for rehearsals, Nancy found Miss Morris waiting for her with a very severe expression on her face. She had a copy of the evening paper in her hand, and it had been folded back on the society page which sported a photograph of a bright cocktail party attended by a very smart set. Nancy was to the forefront of the photograph.

'Mr Singleton would like a word with you, Nancy,' she said quietly.

The girl's heart jerked and her mouth went dry when she saw the photograph.

'I . . . I'm sorry I'm late, Miss Morris,' she said.

'For the second time in a week. Not good enough, Nancy. You'd better go straight through to Mr Singleton's office.'

Mr Singleton was signing one or two letters, but he asked Nancy to shut the door and come and sit down. Presently he looked up and regarded her levelly.

'Are you happy with us, Nancy?' he asked pleasantly.

'Oh yes, very happy,' she assured him eagerly.

'Yet you can't wait to get away each night and seek a rather different form of entertainment. Already you've got tired lines under your eyes and your skin is a poor colour. It doesn't take long for a girl to lose her looks if she burns the candle at both ends. I promised your mother I'd keep an eye on you, Nancy, but apparently I cannot. I think you'd better go home to Scotland.'

'Oh, no!' The cry burst from Nancy's lips. 'Oh, please, Mr Singleton, I . . . I shan't ever be late again.'

'I seem to remember other promises you made.'

'But I mean it. I really mean it, this

time.' Nancy's eyes were wide with distress. 'I've learned all my new songs, and I know them all. I can sing them . . . '

'Not good enough, Nancy. You're tired. That means a poor performance.'

Nancy looked at him with tragic eyes.

'Can I at least be given a week's notice?' she whispered miserably.

'Very well, you'll work a week's notice,' he agreed. 'Though I expect you to be on time every day and in good form every night. We broadcast again on Sunday, but I expect perfection or Sir John Reith will have something to say.'

'Yes, sir,' mumbled Nancy. She had never felt more alone — or more miserable.

★ ★ ★

Unemployment was as rife in Fairlaw as it was anywhere else, and Maria's heart lay in the theatre rather than the more mundane jobs. She had taken to sending off letters which, she said, were applications for jobs. It was only when she attended an interview which proved successful, that Geraldine realised what kind of job it was.

'It is the theatre in Edinburgh,' Maria told her proudly.

'I have to start very low, but the job is in the Lauderdale Theatre in Edinburgh and they are doing a play by George Bernard Shaw. I expect I sweep up floors and make the tea. But just think! I shall see Terry often and often!'

Maria was ecstatic and Geraldine's heart plummeted. Terry was having to work very hard in order to complete his training. What would happen when Maria went to Edinburgh?

Geraldine had never known the house so quiet, now that Nancy, Terry and Maria had all gone. Only Eleanor remained and even Eleanor was going out quite a lot in the evenings. She did a lot of work for her pupils outside school hours.

Geraldine came home from a Red

Cross meeting in town to see Matt Pollock once again leaving the house. He seemed to lie in wait until she had gone out, thought Geraldine grimly, and suddenly she had had enough.

Nancy had telephoned from London and Geraldine could sense there was something wrong, though Nancy airily assured her that all was well, and she would be broadcasting again on Sunday. Geraldine had tried to contact Maria at the boarding house, but one of the other boarders said she was out with her young 'soldier.' It was what she had feared.

Terry and Maria would be spending all their free time together, yet Terry must surely have other things to do. Geraldine longed for the days when she could discipline her children, and make them behave sensibly.

And now here was Eleanor still seeing a young man who was so unsuitable for her in every way. Geraldine caught up with her in the hall and practically rushed her along to the morning room.

'I want to talk to you, Eleanor,' she said firmly.

The girl looked surprised.

'Is there something wrong, Mummy?'

'Certainly there is. I haven't said too much to you about Matt Pollock because I thought your friendship with him was only a temporary affair. But it appears to go on and on. What do you see in him, Eleanor?'

Eleanor stared at her mother, her eyes full of anger.

'You . . . you actually believe that . . . that I'm emotionally involved with Matt Pollock!' she said. 'You really believe that.'

Geraldine had no intention of being put off.

'I'm not a fool, Eleanor,' she said. 'You can't tell me that you haven't had some special sort of interest in your life recently, and that Matt Pollock has been hanging round here for weeks . . . '

'I was going to have talked to you,

Mummy, when we had the chance to get together, but now I don't think I have to tell you anything.' cried Eleanor, her eyes sparkling with anger. 'How dare you question me like this about . . . about Matt Pollock!'

'Because I thought it was time someone did,' said Geraldine.

But Eleanor had gone to the door with her head held very high, the colour in her cheeks very bright. 'I think it's time I went to bed, Mother,' she said quietly. 'Oh, by the way, could you please telephone Alex Kinloch? He wants to speak with you. Also Granny would like to see him. Her hip bone is giving her pain again.'

And then she was gone, leaving her mother alone and confused.

Gathering her thoughts she telephoned Alex Kinloch and he made an appointment to come to see Mrs Wyllie the following afternoon.

'I've been away,' he explained, 'but I want to see you, too, Geraldine. I want to talk to you.'

'What about?'

'I'll tell you when I see you.'

She put down the receiver and went to bed, her head thumping painfully, her emotions in turmoil.

Seeing Richard Again

Alex Kinloch looked grave after he had examined Constance Wyllie. The disease had a very strong hold now on her hip and all movement was painful. He was doing a lot of research on this at the moment and wondered if an operation would help her, but her general health was not good.

Geraldine was waiting for him in the drawing-room with a tray of tea and cakes on a small table beside her.

'This is lovely,' said Alex. 'You manage to make everything warm and inviting, Geraldine. My life is very dull now.'

'But your work means so much to you.'

'Once I thought it meant everything.' He laid his cup down and reached for her hand. 'Now I know it doesn't. When I'm away from you, I . . . realise that

I'm only half alive. I love you, Geraldine. Sometimes I think I must have loved you for a very long time, but it's only now that I can ask you to marry me. I want you very much for my wife.'

Geraldine's cheeks coloured. Somehow she had been aware that one day she might have to face this moment, but now that it was upon her, she hardly knew how to answer. She was very fond of Alex Kinloch. She admired him in every way. But was she in love with him?

The newspaper photograph of Richard Ransome kept coming into her mind, but she forced it back. She had no place in Richard's life now. Her life was here in Fairlaw.

'I don't want your answer now, Geraldine,' he was saying. 'It's only correct that you should think it over. You have many things to consider. I just want you to know that I do love you, my dear.'

'Oh, Alex . . . yes, I'll think it over,'

she agreed. Suddenly she was aware of Jenny Muir coming into the room in a rush. Her face was white and her eyes went from Geraldine to Alex Kinloch.

'Could you come upstairs, Mrs Geraldine?' she asked urgently. 'And the doctor. Mrs Wyllie doesn't look at all well.'

Together Geraldine and Alex raced up the stairs.

Stephen Wyllie stood by his wife's bed, her hand in his, but there was tragedy in his eyes as he turned towards Geraldine.

'I ... I think she's gone,' he whispered. 'I think she's left me.'

Alex stepped forward and gently examined Mrs Wyllie, then he turned and nodded quietly to Geraldine, who put a hand on Stephen Wyllie's arm. For a while they stood together, saying goodbye to a much-loved lady, while the tears flowed freely. Neither Geraldine nor the old man tried to hide their grief.

'She was in great pain,' Alex Kinloch

said gently. 'She'll be at peace now.'

As the weeks after Mrs Wyllie's funeral passed, Geraldine began to realise that she was once again tied very much to Hillcrest.

Nancy, subdued after Mrs Wyllie's death, had been given another chance from a sympathetic Nat Singleton.

Eleanor seemed to find her solace in taking on even more work among her guides and arranging little outings for her pupils.

'It's a waste of her lovely youth,' Geraldine told Alex when they met again after the house was back to normal.

'It's what she wants to do, Geraldine.'

'Well, it's not what I want her to do. She's even transferred her care and concern for her grandmother to her grandfather, and that's my responsibility. Oh dear . . . that reminds me, Alex . . . '

'I know what you're going to say,' he told her. 'You can't think about marrying me until Mr Wyllie has got over his wife's death.'

Geraldine bit her lip. Alex was being very understanding and her heart was warm with the love she felt for him. She was grateful that he didn't expect a quick answer to his proposal, but wasn't there, in her heart of hearts, a little bit of relief, too? She loved him, but she was not passionately in love with him.

Yet how glad she was that he hadn't gone out of her life.

★   ★   ★

Terry and Maria had continued to see one another as often as possible after the German girl had settled down to work at the Lauderdale Theatre. For Terry, the weeks were passing in a haze of delight. On one of her dates he was disappointed when Maria wasn't waiting for him as usual. Where was she, he wondered. Her work at the theatre should have been finished long ago.

Terry's sense of loss was so great that

he was almost frightened. The months seemed to pass too slowly. It was now the spring of 1937 and he still had many months of training ahead of him. He wanted Maria now. He walked along to the Lauderdale Theatre and learned that a message had been left with the doorman. Maria couldn't see him, but she would see him as usual the following day and explain then.

Terry had no choice but to return to barracks.

The following day, he found that his name was on the Special Duties roster and he tried, frantically, to arrange a swop, but without success. Well, if no-one could help him out he would have to take more drastic measures. He carried out the duties allotted to him as far as possible, then he went absent without leave. With luck on his side, he might never be found out.

Maria was ecstatic with happiness when he met her at the boarding house. 'There is to be a new play at the Lauderdale,' she told Terry, 'called

'Paris Mode'. Today I do the rehearsals for Saturday. I am the French maid. I am not good with the French accent, but I speak French well and I make a better French maid than Janette Strange, so I get the part.'

Terry did not know whether to be glad or sorry to hear this news. Now she would be on the stage, and he would see less of her. Besides, he was still annoyed with her for not keeping their date the previous evening.

'Where were you?' he demanded.

'But, darling, I am telling you,' Maria said patiently. 'I am having the audition and I get the part, I am so happy.' She hugged him. 'Tonight we celebrate,' she said, 'and I will read the part to you and you will listen to me saying the lines.'

'I have to get back to my unit,' he told her, and she frowned. But already Terry was feeling more nervous than usual about taking leave of absence. There was no-one at all to cover for him.

'You do not like I go on the stage,'

she accused. 'You do not wish me to be a star. You just want a wife when you become a real soldier, and I shall be an Army wife — a hausfrau.'

'I can't talk about it now,' said Terry. 'I've really got to get back to my unit.'

'You never rush back before — only now when I tell you I am an actress. I want you to kiss me and tell me you're glad — '

Terry swept her into his arms and kissed her, but she could sense his uneasiness.

'You are jealous!' she accused.

'Oh, Maria darling . . . I should be on duty.'

'But you say it is always all right, not like Germany.'

'Yes, but I'm not supposed to be here. I must get back.'

'You will watch me on Saturday?'

'Of course. I'll bring flowers for the birth of a new star.'

She laughed with delight, but her eyes sobered as she watched him hurrying away.

Terry learned that his commanding officer wished to see him as soon as he returned to barracks, and he was quaking as he walked along to the company office.

The officer was a tall man with close-cropped grey hair.

'This is not the first time you have been away from barracks without leave, Wyllie,' he snapped. 'Though the last time it appears you swapped duties with a friend. I did not approve, but you were given the benefit of the doubt. Now I understand you are seeing a girl in Edinburgh.'

'My fiancée, sir,' Terry explained to the C.O.

The eyes raked over him.

'It will be some time before you can marry.'

'Yes, sir.'

'Who is the girl?' The officer was giving Terry no mercy.

'Maria Fischer, sir. She . . . she's German.'

'German!'

'Yes, sir. As a matter of fact,' Terry went on, 'she had to get out of Germany, and I helped her. It was a nasty affair, sir.'

'I don't think you need tell me more, Wyllie, at least not at this moment,' he said icily. 'I shouldn't have to remind you that you are training to become an officer in His Majesty's Forces, and you have been absenting yourself from duty. I think further consideration must be given to your position here, Wyllie, but in the meantime you are confined to barracks. Is that understood?'

'Yes, sir,' Terry croaked.

He marched out of Company Office, his face pale with shock. Not only was his whole career in doubt, he wouldn't be able to see Maria on Saturday. He thought of their earlier disagreement and his heart sank. If he didn't turn up, she would be absolutely furious.

★ ★ ★

As the weather warmed for spring, Eleanor found herself more and more busy with extra-curricular activities at school. She was involved in the elaborate preparations to celebrate the Coronation of King George VI and Queen Elizabeth in May. A gala day was to be held in the big park in Fairlaw and every child was to be presented with a Coronation mug and a bag containing sandwiches, cakes and biscuits. Eleanor was organising games, competitions and a fancy dress parade.

'You could judge that, Mother,' she suggested to Geraldine.

'Oh no, darling, not if you're organising it,' Geraldine objected.

'What about Alex Kinloch?' Eleanor suggested.

'Perhaps, but I would have thought Mrs Ritchie, the provost's wife, was the obvious choice.' Geraldine's voice was thoughtful.

Stephen Wyllie was a little stronger these days. Perhaps he could be left for a day or two with Eleanor and Jenny

Muir, and she could go to London for the Coronation. She wanted to see Nancy again, and especially she wanted to meet this newspaper man, Jonathan Duke who was creeping into every one of Nancy's letters.

Geraldine sighed. Nancy had been so much more subdued these past few months. Terry, too, was keeping himself rather quiet and on her last visit to Edinburgh, she found Maria full of excitement about her rôle in 'Paris Mode.' But there had been a nervous evasion in her when Terry's name came up.

Finally, it was Eleanor who persuaded her mother to go to London for the Coronation, and suddenly Geraldine was happy and excited again as she made plans to stay with Aunt Margaret.

Eleanor was receiving letters with an Ayr postmark and Geraldine desperately wanted to know who they were from. But ever since she had asked her elder daughter about Matt Pollock, a barrier seemed to have grown up between them. Eleanor would confide in her in her own good time, she hoped.

Nancy was delighted to see her mother again, and she managed to squeeze in enough time from rehearsals to meet the train.

'Oh, Mummy, it's so good to see you!' she cried. 'Isn't it exciting? The Coronation, I mean. They're having a special party at the Marchand Hotel on Coronation night, and I'm hoping you'll come with Aunt Margaret, and that Jonathan can come, too.'

'Ah yes . . . Jonathan.' Geraldine's eyes were speculative. Nancy looked very well. There was a more mature air about her. Geraldine suspected that Jonathan Duke was largely responsible for this.

'He might not be able to come, of course,' Nancy went on. 'He's a newshound now. That comes first, every time.'

Geraldine's eyes sharpened as she glanced at her daughter. They had taken a taxi from the station and were now turning the corner into the familiar streets of London which she loved so much.

She gazed with admiration at the variety of decorations strung across the streets as the taxi made its way to Mountjoy Terrace.

Suddenly she was transported back to that other royal occasion when the new King and Queen were married, and her visit to London at that time. Her thoughts went to Richard Ransome. Should she go to see him at the Belvedere, or was it wiser to stay away from him? She would like to see him again . . .

A few minutes later she was at Mountjoy Terrace, and in Aunt Margaret's arms.

Jonathan Duke had managed to obtain seats for Nancy, Geraldine and Aunt Margaret, overlooking part of the Coronation route. Geraldine took to him at once, but assured herself that she would reserve judgment until she got to know him better. He had already written an article for his paper, capturing all the excitement of the special trains which were bringing hundreds of people to London.

'Millions, really,' Jonathan said. 'A million seats and twenty million people to sit on them!' He grinned.

At the party in the Marchand Hotel, Geraldine and Aunt Margaret listened with great pride as Nancy led the guests in singing patriotic songs.

But already Jonathan had slipped away. He had work to do, even on Coronation Day, and Nancy seemed untroubled as they walked towards Mountjoy Terrace, until they could find a taxi. There was a bus strike and thousands of people were also walking home.

'Do you like Jonathan, Mummy?' Nancy asked. 'It's important, you see. I'm going to marry him one day, you know,' she revealed.

'When he has time,' Geraldine blurted out, then bit her lip. 'Oh dear, that slipped out, darling, but you must admit that he tends to be working most of the time.'

'I don't care,' Nancy said. 'I love him. We only want a quiet wedding when the time comes. No fuss. Oh, by the way, Richard Ransome was in the hotel one night last week. His new show is a great success.'

'I am glad,' Geraldine replied noncommittally.

'He was with his leading lady, Eve Tarrant. She's very glamorous.'

'I know. I've seen pictures.'

Suddenly a little of the day's happiness had drained away.

* * *

Geraldine had decided to go home without seeing Richard, but he telephoned Aunt Margaret's house the following day, and Aunt Margaret happily handed over the receiver.

'Yes, she's here, Richard,' she told him. 'You've guessed correctly.'

'Why didn't you get in touch with me?' he asked when Geraldine took the receiver. 'I tried to telephone you but

I've been so busy.'

'I'm glad you're such a success, Richard,' Geraldine said politely.

'What's wrong?' he asked. 'You sound different. Look, it's so difficult for me to get away. Couldn't you come round and see me at the theatre? I'll leave a ticket for you.'

'Very well,' she agreed. 'I'll be glad to come, Richard.'

Geraldine felt like a young girl again as she prepared to go to the Belvedere Theatre. She chose a heavy silk gown with a white stole, and her hair looked dark and shining as she brushed it into soft waves. On impulse she touched up her face with make-up and the result was quite astonishing.

She was in time to watch Richard's new show, and as she sat watching the performance, Geraldine felt some of her confidence draining away. Eve Tarrant was very lovely, and Richard looked better than ever. He sang and danced to a thunder of applause. At the final curtain call, he looked towards where

Geraldine was sitting and slowly she rose to her feet and made her way backstage.

Richard lost no time in enveloping her in his arms, and kissing her warmly. 'You look wonderful, Geraldine,' he told her. 'I've heard all the family news from Nancy, you know. I was very sorry to hear about your mother-in-law. I've been hoping to get in touch with you ever since.'

Richad had poured out two glasses of wine, and handed one to her. 'To us,' he said, raising his glass.

'To us,' she repeated, though her eyes were speculative as she looked at him. He never changed, she thought, and she realised how very dear to her he was — perhaps he was even more than that. He made her feel more alive than anyone she knew.

'What are your plans now, Geraldine?' he was asking. 'Your family have grown up and are living their own lives. What about you? Have you considered a return to London?'

She sipped her wine, then put down the glass. 'Laurence's father is still at Fairlaw,' she said quietly. 'He's no longer the strong man he used to be.'

He stared at her, then turned away. 'I see. You're still tied to your home in Scotland.'

'What about you?' she asked. 'I've seen the papers — your photograph . . . with Eve Tarrant.'

He turned swiftly to look at her. 'Would you mind that, Geraldine? Would you care if I took another woman?' Suddenly he had pulled her into his arms and was kissing her as he had kissed her so many years ago. 'There are still so many years ahead, Geraldine,' he whispered. 'Must we waste them apart?'

For a while she remained in his arms, then they heard the sound of a woman's light voice, calling his name, and Geraldine pulled herself out of his arms.

'I must go,' she said quickly. 'I have to go home tomorrow.'

'I'll be in touch,' he promised. 'If you want to hear from me, that is.'

She did not reply, but as the taxi returned her to Mountjoy Terrace, she knew that the kind of love she had for Richard was, indeed, very different from the fond affection she felt for Alex Kinloch.

Eleanor And Paul

Geraldine left for Fairlaw next day. Eleanor was due to return to teaching and Stephen Wyllie could no longer be left unattended for any length of time. Nancy had wanted to talk over her future plans with Jonathan, but Geraldine's mind was too full of Richard to listen with close attention and sympathy.

'Later,' she told Nancy. 'You're very young, darling. There's plenty of time for you to think about marriage. From what you tell me, it's not at all settled in any case.'

'It will be.' Nancy looked mulish. 'Can't we talk about it?'

'Certainly. I . . . I might want to come to London a little more often. I will see you very soon again, dear.'

The train journey seemed more tedious than usual, and Geraldine was tired as she walked in the door at Hillcrest. Suddenly Eleanor was running to meet her across the hall.

'Oh, Mummy,' she said. 'I've just had a telephone call from Maria. She hasn't seen Terry for days and days . . . '

Geraldine put down her small case and removed her hat.

'If there was anything wrong with Terry, we would have been told by now,' she said decisively. 'I've no doubt his duties have been changed. Maria will have to get used to the fact that an officer in training cannot always please himself. I'd love some tea, Eleanor.'

'I'll get it. She sounded so upset, that's all.'

Meanwhile, Maria was sitting in the boarding-house, her mouth drooping with disappointment, and growing anxiety, an anxiety which had prompted her to rush out to the telephone and ring up Hillcrest. She had waited with eagerness for Terry to turn up, as usual, and for him to accompany her to the Lauderdale Theatre and watch her playing her very first part as an actress. He had promised her flowers, and Terry always kept his promises.

After yet another day without news, Maria decided she must go out to the barracks and try to see Terry, or find out where he was.

The Officers' Training Unit was a fine Georgian building with a handsome entrance. There was a large parade ground with several smaller buildings beyond the main one, the whole enclosed behind very high railings with a guard house near the main gate.

Several young trainee officers were marching in and out, and one or two turned to look at her with curiosity before one of them walked towards her.

'Can I help you, miss?' he asked.

'I must see someone,' she said nervously. 'I am looking for Terence Wyllie.'

'Wyllie?' The young officer frowned then turned to his friend. 'Know anyone called Wyllie?'

An older man in the uniform of a private in the Regular Army turned to look at him.

'Lieutenant Wyllie, sir,' he said. 'I know him. He's on jankers.'

'Young lady here to see him,' the officer said.

The older man came to look at Maria. 'You'd better not hang about, miss, and get him into any more trouble.'

'Terry's in trouble?' Maria's eyes went wide with alarm.

'Ay. Some.' The soldier nodded. 'No use hiding it. I work in the cook-house and — '

'He peels the potato mountain,' Maria broke in.

'Something like that. Look, miss, if you want to see him for five minutes. I'll show you where to wait, then I'll get him to talk to you. But he can't leave Barracks. There's a wee place round the back where you can be together and I'll watch out for him. The Duty Officer will be having his tea. But it's five

116

minutes only . . . '

It seemed a long time before Terry came to find Maria in a quiet corner of the grounds near a shrubbery.

'Maria? Darling?' he said.

'I'm here, Terry.' She had managed to squeeze through the railings and flew into his arms. 'There's not much time,' she said urgently. 'The soldier said so. Oh, Terry, you are in trouble with your commander because of me.'

'Because of my own stupidity.' Terry said. 'Don't blame yourself, darling. I tried to get a message to you, but no luck.'

'And now they keep you in here, like in prison, though you say it is not like Germany. Oh, Terry, I'm so . . . so afraid. They are angry with you because of me. That's it, is it not?' Her big eyes were moist with tears as she stared at him.

'They'll get over it.'

'So you do not deny it! They are angry with you because of me, because I am German. If I were a Scottish girl, they would not mind.'

'Oh yes they would!' he replied with a half smile on his lips. 'Nationality is nothing to do with it!'

'Oh, you joke about it.' She stroked his face. 'But it's true, Terry. Armies are all the same. Always it is discipline. They will not believe that there are Germans who do not want war and that many of us are now in Britain, or in America, because we do not wish to stay in Germany.'

'I know. I told them that, but — ' Terry broke off, biting his lip.

'Darling Terry, I cannot do this to you. Always I would spoil your life. I will go to London where you will not find me and you can tell your commander that I have gone out of your life.'

'Maria! For goodness' sake, don't do that!' Terry replied desperately. 'I can't get out of here at the moment, or I'd take you straight home.'

'I would not go,' she said proudly. 'I have been enough trial to your mother and your family, and you. We are not engaged.' She tugged at her ring, tears beginning to spill down her cheeks.

'No!' he cried. 'Maria, I love you. Don't take off your ring.'

'Yes. I must go. It is the only way.' She was tugging at her ring, but it stuck on her finger. A moment later there was a long, low whistle from somewhere behind them. 'That is the signal,' she said. 'Your officer comes looking for you. I go now, Terry.'

She reached up swiftly and kissed him on the lips, then she slid towards the gap in the railings. 'I send back your ring — '

'No! I don't want it back. Maria, don't take it off — '

'I send it back. Someday, when you are a fine officer, you will be glad.' Suddenly she was gone.

She couldn't mean it, Terry told himself.

★ ★ ★

A few days later Geraldine was startled to see a taxi drawing up outside the door, and Terry emerging with all his luggage.

'Terry! What are you doing home at this time, and where have you been, darling? I've been trying so hard to get in touch with you. It's lovely to see you, though. Have you been on a special course, and are now having leave?'

Terry greeted her with a quick kiss, then walked straight through to the sitting-room, leaving his things in the hall.

Geraldine followed him.

'You might as well know straight-away,' he told her jerkily. 'I . . . I've been sent down. I've been put off the course.'

Geraldine's mouth fell open. It had always been such a passion with Terry to be an army officer like his father. Why, even his visit to Berlin had been prompted by this very keen interest.

Berlin! Geraldine's thoughts immediately went to Maria.

'Have you seen Maria?' she asked. 'She was trying to get in touch with you here.'

'I've seen her,' Terry replied curtly.

'Was it because she's German that you got put off the course?' Geraldine pursued.

'It was because I went absent without leave. I had to try to see her as often as I could. I . . . I was all she had . . . '

'Then she's still in Edinburgh?'

'No. She . . . she thought she was ruining my career, so she walked out on everything, her very first acting role that she was so proud of, the boarding house she liked so much, and . . . and me.' He stared at his mother. 'She walked out on me, though she loves me, I know she loves me. She's gone to London with hardly anything in her pocket, to try to make another new beginning in order to save my career. She did it for me. Only it was all for nothing. They've heaved me out anyway.'

Terry sat down miserably on the settee.

'I'm sorry things have turned out badly for you, darling,' Geraldine said. 'But it seems to me that much of it is your own fault. As for Maria, no doubt she'll get in touch with you again, in her own good time.'

Terry scowled. No-one really understood about Maria. Not even his mother. He loved Maria, but she had walked out on him for nothing. Well, now he would be like Maria and make a new life for himself.

* * *

Nancy missed her mother after Geraldine had gone home. She was gaining experience and her performance with the orchestra was excellent, but she had wanted to talk to her mother about Jonathan, and try to get her to understand that theirs was not a conventional love affair.

Nancy hardly knew when she first

started to fall in love with Jonathan, and there had never been any question of an engagement between them. When the time was ripe, they would slip away quietly and get married. Already she knew that she couldn't visualise life with any other man.

'It'll take a few years for us to build a nest for ourselves, young Wyllie.' Jonathan had said to her one day as he saw her home to Aunt Margaret's. 'Nice house this. It seems a long time since I lived in what you could call a real home — I lost my mother in that flu epidemic after the war, and my father and I rubbed along as best we could. Now he's gone off to New Zealand to work on a newspaper. It's in the blood, young Wyllie. We crawl along the streets, with our noses to the ground, tracking down the odd sensation. That's no life for a young wife.'

'No, it isn't,' Nancy agreed serenely.

'The trouble is, I'm a healthy young chap and I've fallen in love with Nancy Wyllie.'

'Oh, Jonathan!' Nancy laughed. 'I do love you.'

'It's crazy, isn't it?' he asked, kissing her. 'And it's no life for a girl, keeping house for a fellow who lives in the streets, and in the buses, trams, trains and even aeroplanes.'

'Yes, but I have my own career, darling. Don't forget that. I wouldn't be sitting bored at home, darning your socks. I would be singing with the orchestra, and we would be together whenever we could manage it.'

'True. A nice little flat in London, perhaps. Not bad. But your folk would want a big wedding, and — '

'And half an hour before the service, Mussolini would decide to come to Britain for a holiday!' Nancy interrupted.

'Right. You're quick on the understanding, young Wyllie.'

'Then we do get married?'

'Certainly. When we can fit it in. What's wrong? What's the joke?'

Nancy was laughing helplessly, wondering what her mother would say if she could hear their conversation!

'No joke. Oh, Jonathan, darling, are you sure you love me?'

'Haven't I just said so? I love you.' He folded her in his arms as she kissed him and ran her fingers through his hair. He kissed her again and they clung together, so that Jonathan put her away from him rather unsteadily.

'There's a lot to do. We must find that flat, Nancy darling, and . . . ' He looked at his watch. 'I . . . '

'Time for you to go,' she said, her eyes dancing. It didn't matter that he had to tear himself away from her. He loved her. That was all that mattered.

Geraldine had not pondered too deeply on Nancy's affairs in London. Now that she was home again in Fairlaw, it was Eleanor and Terry who occupied most of her thoughts. Her son was providing her with problems of a very different kind. He had always lived a busy social life but now it seemed there were not enough hours in the day for all he wanted to do.

Geraldine might have been glad to see him going out and enjoying himself with some nice local girl, but instead he seemed to take out a different girl every week.

The registered post had brought a small package for him, and when he opened it, he found that it contained Maria's ring and a small note which told him to forget her, and to forgive her. Swiftly he had crossed to his desk and dropped the ring into the top drawer.

'Don't wait up for me, Mother,' he told her. 'I may be late tonight.'

Eleanor had brought in the post that morning, and she had looked disappointed when there was nothing for her. But the following morning brought the usual letter with the Ayr postmark, and Geraldine watched her daughter's eyes beginning to sparkle.

It was time she knew a little more about the writer of the letter, she decided firmly. Eleanor had been receiving them for months, ever since she had taken her guides to Ayr, Geraldine realised. And it was almost time for her to go back to camp again!

★   ★   ★

Geraldine got the chance to speak to Eleanor one Saturday afternoon when she opted out of a tennis match in order to start her preparations for going to camp. Lists of suitable clothing must be made, and her first-aid kit had to be brought up to date.

'I expect your friend from Ayr will be available if you need any help, dear,' Geraldine said pleasantly.

'What . . . what friend?' Eleanor flushed scarlet.

'Oh, come now, I'm not a fool,' her mother replied briskly. 'You can't always smuggle those letters out of sight. It isn't hard to guess that they are from a man friend, though I'm rather curious, and perhaps even a little concerned, that you don't appear to be willing, or able, to invite him home for dinner. You . . . you aren't ashamed of him, are you?'

'Of course not!' Eleanor cried. 'He's a wonderful man!'

'Then there is someone,' Geraldine said triumphantly, and Eleanor flushed, biting her lip.

'His name's Paul Bryden,' she said slowly. 'He works in a bank in Ayr, and he . . . he lives in the house next to the field we hire for the guide camp. Paul was very helpful with any problems which came up.' She stared at her mother, then caught her arm. 'We're only friends, Mummy, honestly. We only saw each other about half a dozen times, then I wrote to thank Paul and he wrote back and . . . and somehow we have become penfriends, that's all.'

'Can't you invite him to dinner one weekend?' Geraldine asked. 'He could stay overnight . . . '

'He needn't, his father lets him use his car,' Eleanor said swiftly.

'There you are then,' her mother said. 'Invite him for next Saturday.'

'I'll think about it,' Eleanor said, biting her lip. 'I . . . I'll let you know, Mummy.'

Eleanor went up to her room and took out Paul's latest letter.

I'm looking forward so much to the time when you will be bringing your guides back to camp, he wrote. I hope I shall see you as much as possible. It's a delight to me that we have so much in common, Eleanor, and can share so many simple pleasures. I have set several books aside for you to read, and perhaps you will tell me if you like Anthony Adverse, or if no book can ever be the equal of Gone With The Wind. I know how responsible you feel for your young guides, but perhaps this time we might spend an hour or two together one evening?

Eleanor laid the letter aside and slowly reached for her writing case. If she didn't invite Paul, her mother would wonder if there was something wrong with him. Biting her lip, Eleanor swiftly penned the invitation, then ran downstairs and went to post her letter before she could change her mind. But she would make sure that Paul knew she was only being friendly. He must not get the wrong idea.

Not for the first time, Geraldine felt that she wanted to shake her children by the shoulders. She had been delighted when the young man, Paul Bryden, wrote a charming letter of acceptance to dinner, a letter which had sent Eleanor behind a wall of reserve.

Geraldine had also asked Terry if he would be joining the family for dinner, and a look in his mother's eyes convinced him that it would be expedient for him to be part of the family dinner party. Besides, he rather wanted to meet Eleanor's boyfriend, and size up what sort of chap he was.

As far as Geraldine was concerned, Paul was everything she could have desired for Eleanor. He was tall and nice looking without being too hand-some. He had fair curly hair and bright blue eyes in a weather-beaten face. One of his hobbies was sailing, but he also liked walking and playing tennis.

Geraldine had encouraged Eleanor to see the young man away in his father's car, but Eleanor had spent very little time alone with Paul Bryden. Instead she had slipped back indoors and had run upstairs to bed. Her mother had not seen her tears, and would never have understood how Eleanor felt.

She had wanted Paul to be first to take her out. Now her mother had forced the initiative on to her. Everything was spoiled, thought Eleanor — everything.

★   ★   ★

Geraldine, beyond a few words of approval, forgot about Paul Bryden as the weeks began to pass again. She was very busy organising her Red Cross work and it seemed there was much to

131

be done in all her voluntary work.

Many preventative measures were now being taken in case Britain was forced into war with Germany, and children were being fitted with gas masks and plans mooted for their evacuation from cities and towns, should the unthinkable really happen.

It meant a lot of work for a lot of people and Geraldine threw herself into all that was required to be done with energy and enthusiasm. She deplored the way Terry was wasting his time and even suggested that he could retrieve some of his disappointment over the Army by joining the Territorials.

'You must be joking!' Terry retorted. 'They threw me out, then you expect me to go and do my bit elsewhere! I was a good officer, Mother . . . or I would have been. I was always near the top of my class in the examinations.'

'A good officer is made of better stuff than mere examination results,' Geraldine reasoned with a sigh.

She could do with hearing from Alex

again, but he, too, was kept busy. Richard rang from London and Geraldine's heart leapt at the sound of his voice, quite clear over the phone. 'Aren't you coming back to London soon?' he asked her bluntly.

'Not at the moment, Richard.'

'What's stopping you?'

Everything, Geraldine thought — Terry, Eleanor, old Mr Wyllie and perhaps, most of all, Richard himself.

'Let me know when you can,' he urged. 'I want to see you.'

'Very well. I'll tell you when.'

Nancy was glad her mother hadn't managed to come back to London. Occasionally her conscience bothered her not a little as she and Jonathan made their own plans. Nancy knew that her family would be hurt, but she had a whole lifetime of living ahead of her, and coolly and deliberately she weighed up her plans and decided that Jonathan came first.

The family would soon get used to the idea of her marriage, and would accept it. But if she told her mother and Eleanor, then she would be talked into having a proper wedding in no time, with Eleanor as bridesmaid, and her mother and Aunt Margaret having a good cry. Jonathan would hate it.

Aunt Margaret! Nancy bit her lip. She had a bad conscience over Aunt Margaret. Soon the orchestra was going to Eastbourne for a few months, and Nancy had already told Aunt Margaret she would be leaving Mountjoy Terrace for a few weeks to go there. But she had not told the old lady that she wouldn't be coming back. She and Jonathan would be married quietly and would spend their honeymoon in Eastbourne. Aunt Margaret knew nothing of this.

On the following Saturday morning Nancy left Mountjoy Terrace in a taxi containing considerable luggage, mainly clothes. She hugged Aunt Margaret and kissed her several times.

'I've loved it here . . . in London. I mean,' she said. 'I expect I shall love Eastbourne, too. Oh, Aunt Margaret, just remember that I love you.'

'And I you, my dear,' Aunt Margaret said, looking at her levelly. 'Nancy, are you really — '

'Here's my taxi, darling,' Nancy interrupted. 'I've got to go!'

Aunt Margaret watched her go then sat down to ponder the matter deeply. She was not as gullible as Nancy imagined and the girl showed all the signs of an elopement. Yet . . . what if she was wrong?

A Sad Loss

Nancy and Jonathan's honeymoon at Eastbourne lasted for three deliriously happy days. Jonathan rang his newspaper office each evening, but the news was such that they could retire early and spend their precious hours together.

On the third night, Nancy left Jonathan at the telephone and walked upstairs to their room. She was beginning to save money from her earnings and had bought the most beautiful negligee she'd been able to find. As she brushed out her honey-gold curls, she reflected that she had never felt better or happier in her whole life.

She glanced at her watch, deciding that Jonathan had been a long time, when suddenly the bedroom door flew open and he rushed in, his eyes brilliant with excitement.

'I've been recalled,' he told her breathlessly. 'Back to London. Sorry, darling, but I've got to pack. Something really big is breaking — really momentous . . . Got to be on hand . . . ' He began to throw his clothes into a suitcase.

'Jonathan? You can't go and leave me like this! You just can't!'

'Sorry, darling,' he told her. 'I can't help it. This is real news. Chamberlain is flying to Munich to meet Hitler. It's momentous! I've got to be on hand when he returns you see, Nancy.'

'I can't come with you,' she said, flags of colour in her cheeks. 'I've got a few more weeks yet with the orchestra here.'

'You know what the job entails, darling,' he said, and the note in his voice hardened. 'Don't make it difficult. I'll just be in time for the last train. I'll be in touch. 'Bye, darling.'

When her sobs had eased, Nancy looked at the time. It was still fairly early and her mother would not yet be in bed. She had sent her a telegram, followed by a glowing letter full of her own happiness.

Quickly she tugged off her lovely negligee and put on her blouse and skirt, then ran downstairs to the telephone.

Geraldine listened with growing alarm and consternation to Nancy's babbled story, her heart aching for the girl who was still very much her baby.

But now Nancy was grown up. She had made her own decision when she and Jonathan married in this way.

'I'm sorry you've been parted so soon, darling,' she said quietly. 'But I'm sure you'll cope very well, Nancy.'

'But, Mummy . . . ' Nancy recoiled from the coolness in her mother's tone. 'Are you angry with me for not telling you about the wedding? Couldn't you find time to come to see me?'

'No, darling, I'm sorry. Your grandfather needs me.' She must not be tempted to respond to Nancy's pleading. 'As for your wedding, well, you made your own decision over that.'

'All right, Mummy.' Nancy sighed faintly.

'Good-night.' Geraldine hung up the telephone.

This time, Nancy had to stand on her own feet.

Having completed her stint with the orchestra in Eastbourne, Nancy returned to London to live in her new flat. She had made a record with the orchestra and all the family had listened proudly to it being played on the radio.

Geraldine would have gone to London to see Nancy and Jonathan but she felt she still couldn't leave old Mr Wyllie. Only she was aware of how much his body shook nowadays when he mounted the stairs to bed, and how much effort he put in to appearing as strong as ever in front of his grandchildren.

He read 'Picture Post' and argued with Terry over many of the articles and pictures.

'Women with their skirts above their knees.' He snorted, and glowered at Terry's grin. 'Pictures taken by staff photographers . . . German refugees, they say.'

Terry's brows darkened. 'Good luck to them, I say,' he retorted. He had tried hard to find Maria but she had vanished out of his life.

In fact, the passing of time had helped to ease his sore heart, but he had no idea what he wanted to do with his future.

Geraldine was making out new lists of accommodation for evacuees in the study the following Friday afternoon when Jenny Muir came to tell her that Mr and Mrs Maguire had called to see her with their daughter, Helen.

'Mr and Mrs Maguire?' Geraldine echoed, puzzled.

'They live out in the Newtown district,' Jenny prompted helpfully. 'He's Maguire the optician in the High Street.'

'Oh, of course.' Geraldine said, standing up. 'It will be something to do with the evacuees, I expect. Are they in the sitting-room, Jenny? Can you bring a tray of tea and biscuits?'

'Right away,' Jenny promised.

Geraldine stopped short, however, when she entered the sitting-room to see that Helen Maguire's eyes were swollen with tears and her parents were looking at Geraldine with undisguised hostility.

'Good afternoon,' Geraldine began politely. 'How nice of you to call — '

'It isn't a social visit,' Mr Maguire interrupted. 'At least, not as such. We really came to see your son, but I understand he's not in at the moment.'

'No. He — he's in Edinburgh today,' Geraldine explained.

'Then we'll return another day when he is here,' he said.

The door opened and Jenny came in, bearing a tray.

'Look, here's some tea,' Geraldine said. 'Why don't you sit down and we can talk over any problem,' she suggested.

'We've had tea, thank you, Mrs Wyllie,' Mrs Maguire said very politely.

'Come along, Helen.'

'We'll return to see Terry soon,' Mr Maguire said, turning to Geraldine, 'but I must say he's not a very responsible young man. He should be made to see the consequences of his behaviour.'

Geraldine's eyes met Jenny's as she returned to the sitting-room, where her father-in-law was already seated.

'We'll not judge the boy until we hear what he has to say for himself,' Stephen Wyllie said, rather to Geraldine's surprise.

'Yes, Father,' Geraldine said meekly. But even as she drank her tea, she could see the tear-stained face of Helen Maguire.

Terry had been to a friend's twenty-first birthday party and it was very late when he returned home. His family had become used to his late nights and normally everyone was in bed when he let himself into the house, but tonight Geraldine was waiting for him.

'In here, Terry,' she said, tight-lipped.

'Your grandfather has just gone up. We both waited up as long as we could.'

'What's up?' Terry asked, his face going pale with alarm.

'Helen Maguire,' she said. 'And her parents. Does that mean anything to you?'

'What did they say?' he asked.

'They refused to say anything till you were present,' Geraldine told him. 'Terry, I want to hear it from you.'

Terry's eyes had hardened. 'I don't think there's anything to discuss,' he told her coolly.

'Oh yes there is!' Geraldine exclaimed. 'When decent, honourable people bring a weeping girl into my house and ask to see you, there is a great deal to discuss.'

'Apparently you've already decided what it's all about!' Terry shouted. 'I'm accused, tried and condemned without a hearing. Thank you very much. If you don't mind, I'm going to bed.'

'But I want to discuss it! I want to give you that hearing!'

'Well, it's too late! You've obviously made up your mind and as far as I'm concerned, there's nothing to discuss!' Terry walked out of the room and bounded up the stairs.

* * *

Sadly, she climbed the stairs, then peeped into Stephen Wyllie's room. He was propped up on pillows and on the point of dropping off to sleep under his nightly sedation.

'As I thought,' he mumbled. 'I could hear most of it, you know. Wait and see what the boy says . . . '

Geraldine pressed his fingers and stayed with him until he dropped off to sleep.

In the morning, Stephen Wyllie was dead.

In later years, Geraldine always associated the scent of lilies with the funeral of her father-in-law. Stephen Wyllie had been a notable figure all his life in Fairlaw and the floral tributes filled two rooms.

It was also the time when her son Terry grew into a man, and took charge of all proceedings from her nerveless fingers.

Eleanor, too, was deeply upset and it was left to Nancy to take on some of the responsibility for arranging meals for mourners who had travelled some distance. She was an older, more mature Nancy, but she had lost weight. This time, too, Jonathan had come with her and Geraldine found herself responding to him more than she had done on their previous meeting.

Eleanor's tears flowed even faster when she found that, by the terms of her grandfather's will, she had inherited Hillcrest.

Stephen Wyllie had talked this over with Geraldine and had decided that Eleanor was the ideal choice.

'Terry might marry some unsuitable woman,' he had told Geraldine, 'who would want to sell the place. I want you to live here for as long as you wish, my dear, but I also want you to be free to return to London without being encumbered by Hillcrest, if you prefer to do that. Eleanor will take care of it.'

'That's very wise,' Geraldine had agreed.

'Of course, the rest of you will be compensated, and I shall see that Terry can't squander his. Nancy, too. And you, my dear. I shall take care of you.'

⋆   ⋆   ⋆

The long, hot days of August slipped into September, and it was Terry who worried Geraldine most. He was taking his grandfather's death very badly, and Geraldine had been unable to talk to him about Helen Maguire. She learned from Jenny that the Maguires had gone away for a few weeks' holiday, but when she imparted this piece of news to Terry, he merely turned away without speaking.

Germany invaded Poland and on September 3 Eleanor rushed into the study with the news that background music only was being played on the radio and the Prime Minister would speak to the nation at eleven o'clock. It had been a leisurely Sunday and Geraldine called for Terry and Jenny to come to the sitting-room.

Together all four sat round the radio as the Prime Minister explained that an ultimatum had been sent demanding Germany's withdrawal from Poland, otherwise Britain would be in a state of war with Germany. They listened gravely whilst the tired voice told them that Germany had not replied to the ultimatum.

'Everything that I have believed in during my public life has crashed in ruins,' the Prime Minister said, and Geraldine felt that Neville Chamberlain had never been more impressive. 'It is evil things that we shall be fighting against — brute force, bad faith, injustice, oppression and persecution.'

'I'm glad your grandfather didn't live long enough to hear these terrible words,' Geraldine said as she switched off the radio. 'We have a sad task ahead of us.'

'But we shall win, Mummy, shan't we?' Eleanor asked.

'Of course we shall,' Geraldine countered stoutly. 'We shall win, but it will be a hard task.'

Terry stared at her almost unseeingly. He might have been a fully-fledged officer by now if he hadn't behaved so stupidly, especially over Maria. Maria!

'What will become of Maria?' he asked. 'Surely they won't send her home!'

'Of course not,' Geraldine said. 'I'm more worried about Nancy and Jonathan — and Aunt Margaret. What if there are air raids?'

She telephoned Nancy, then Aunt Margaret.

'No need to worry, dear,' Aunt Margaret said briskly. 'The air raid warning was only a false alarm.'

'What air raid warning?' Geraldine asked.

'Shortly after war was declared. I

don't think their planes could carry bombs this far, do you?'

Geraldine looked worried as she hung up the telephone.

'There's been a warning already,' she told Terry. 'But it was a false alarm. Poor Aunt Margaret forgets about the last war — she's getting old. But the war will be fought in the air, as well as on land and at sea.'

Terry nodded. This time he agreed with his mother.

On the morning that a letter marked OHMS arrived for Geraldine informing her that the German girl she had sponsored when she first arrived in Britain was now in an Internment Camp, Terry volunteered for the Royal Air Force.

'Some say the war will be over in a few months,' he told his mother. 'I shall have to help fight the Germans. I don't want Maria to be held in a place like that.'

'She's probably on the Isle of Man, and that isn't such a hardship.'

'She's still a prisoner, though. Maria will hate that. The authorities are stupid if they just shut her up. She'll be practically bilingual by now. She could be a lot of use to them.'

'I expect they're aware of that,' Geraldine nodded.

When she saw Terry off to report to his unit, Geraldine was torn between pride and apprehension. Terry had seemed to grow up so quickly, and she hardly knew this efficient young man who had left his affairs in such good order at Hillcrest. He had even finally talked to Geraldine about Helen Maguire.

'I've seen the Maguires,' he told her, 'and apologised to Helen in front of her parents. I'm sorry she read so much into our . . . our friendship.'

'Read so much into it?' Geraldine echoed faintly.

'She was engaged to Alan Young but I asked her out on a few occasions. She wasn't wearing a ring or anything — it was apparently being repaired. I didn't realise she and Alan were finally engaged — oh, all right, I had a fairly good idea, but she was pretty and a very good dancer. Only . . . I kissed her a few times and she took it to mean I was in love with her and broke it off with Alan.

'The Maguires and the Youngs have always been friends and Helen's parents were upset about it, especially when Alan Young took it badly. They blamed me. And . . . and, of course, Helen was upset when she found I . . . I didn't really care for her in that way.' Terry looked at his mother, and his eyes were miserable.

'I kept telling myself it wasn't my fault, but it was. Helen and Alan might be happy by now, but for me. I never really loved her, but if I hadn't singled her out for attention, she might not have thought I was serious. Not only that, but I feel it all helped to shorten Grandfather's life . . . '

'Grandfather was a very old man and his health had been failing for some time,' she told him. 'In any case, he knew you were not to be blamed too much. He kept telling me to listen to your story before making judgments. I should have listened to him.'

'Did he really?' Terry's eyes began to clear.

'On my honour,' Geraldine said softly.

'I think he would be glad to know I'm in the RAF,' Terry said. 'I'll give a good account of myself.'

★ ★ ★

Evacuees with labels round their necks poured into Fairlaw from the Glasgow trains, and Geraldine went with Eleanor to collect two mothers with three children, two girls and a boy. Quickly Jenny Muir took charge of the newcomers and sternly passed on the rules of the household, though Geraldine and Eleanor soon let their bewildered guests understand that they were welcome.

In fact, Jenny Muir was glad to have

someone to spoil now that she had lost Mr and Mrs Wyllie and all her 'bairns' were going away. She missed Nancy, and even more so, Terry. He had made her promise to write to him and give him all her news and this she did with unfailing regularity.

'Look, I know you're worried about Nancy,' Eleanor said sympathetically. 'Why don't you go to London to see her and Aunt Margaret. I'm quite capable of carrying on here.'

Eleanor thought her mother looked tired. She had been working very hard on her Women's Voluntary Service work and Eleanor thought a break would do her good.

In any case, Eleanor wanted to do a little thinking on her own for a while. Paul Bryden had joined the Royal Navy and his letters were full of all the warmth and friendship which had coloured their earlier letters to one another.

She had never been sure how she felt about Paul, but now she wanted to see him again and to think about her own future. But she wanted to do it alone.

Geraldine took Eleanor's advice.

Nancy was delighted to see her mother, and proudly took her round the ground-floor flat in Maida Vale which was her home and Jonathan's, and which they could afford with their joint earnings.

'He's still away a great deal,' she told her mother ruefully. 'You know he's now working for a news agency as a war correspondent. That's going to mean front-line stuff for Jonathan.'

Geraldine noted her daughter's quick, nervous movements. She was worrying more about Jonathan than she cared to admit, yet she was also more beautiful than she had ever been. Her young, rounded face had now fined down and she looked arrestingly lovely.

'Why don't you go home for a while?' Geraldine suggested. 'Go to Eleanor. She'd love to have you.'

'Oh no, Mummy! I've got work to do,

you know. Half of the orchestra has joined up, and the rest is broken up into small units. I'll probably be touring the country with a few members of the orchestra to sing in works canteens and small garrison theatres. I'll be too busy to go home to Fairlaw,' she explained.

'Oh, are you planning to see Richard Ransome at all?' she went on. 'He telephoned me, thinking you might be here. He'd tried Hillcrest, but got some stranger . . . '

'One of the evacuees no doubt,' Geraldine put in. Her heart had leaped again at the mention of Richard's name. He had written to her after Stephen Wyllie died, then the war had come. Besides, she was still in mourning.

'I'll get in touch,' Geraldine said.

'Not at the Belvedere. That's been requisitioned for some sort of headquarters, but Aunt Margaret has an address for him when he's not at his flat. Do you really want to go to

Mountjoy Terrace? You can stay here if you like.'

'Not if you're working, dear,' Geraldine pointed out. 'I should be on my own.'

'As you like.' Nancy shrugged, then came to hug her mother. 'Oh, Mummy, surely it will be over soon!' Her voice lowered. 'I want Jonathan home. I need him in my life.'

Echoes of the past came to Geraldine, of the times she'd had to part with Laurence.

'I know, darling,' she said. 'Oh, how I know!'

'. . . Waiting For You'

Aunt Margaret Temple had grown into an old lady.

'I'm so glad to see you, Geraldine,' she said. 'I confess I find all these new regulations for war-time very bewildering. Surely we didn't have this last time, though I forget so easily. My curtain wasn't quite blacked out last week and the warden was very sharp. Oh, by the way, Richard Ransome telephoned, and I told him you were coming to stay. Was that right?'

'Of course.' Geraldine confirmed. 'Don't worry, darling. I'll check the black-out.'

Geraldine rang the number Richard had left with Aunt Margaret, but there was no reply, and her disappointment was so great it was almost painful. It was two evenings later that Richard telephoned, and Geraldine's heart raced as she listened to the sound of his voice again.

'Geraldine!' he exclaimed. 'I thought you'd vanished without trace. I kept telephoning, but you'd either gone, or hadn't yet arrived!'

'You're a bit elusive yourself, Richard,' she said. 'Where are you at the moment?'

'Victoria Station. Look, Geraldine, I haven't got a lot of time. I'm waiting for a special train. Can you meet me here?'

'As soon as I can get there,' she promised.

Richard was looking tired but he hurried forward to meet her.

'We've so little time,' he said urgently. 'Oh, Geraldine, just let me look at you. Either your family needs you or you're in mourning, or I can't even find you. Yet I've wanted you so much. I've been prepared to wait, but suddenly there's no time. We're at war and everyone is in the front line. I . . . I'm going to France.'

They were sitting at a small table in a

quiet corner of the buffet and his voice was lowered so that no-one else could hear.

'I love you so much, Geraldine,' he told her. 'I've loved you all my life. All the years that have gone past were just a time of waiting, waiting for you. I used to tell myself I only wanted your happiness, but the war makes me tell the truth. I don't care about anybody else but us. I want you to marry me right away. I should be back in two weeks. Can you be ready by then?' He grasped her hands. 'I'm not wrong, am I? You do love me, don't you?'

Geraldine had been gazing at him. Suddenly all pretence between them had been removed, and there was only a great love and a desire for one another which had haunted Geraldine for years. No-one else mattered at this moment, no-one but Richard.

'Oh, my darling, yes, yes,' she told him urgently. 'I'll be ready.'

Geraldine returned to Mountjoy Terrace with stars in her eyes, after seeing Richard away at Victoria Station, and she kissed and hugged the old lady.

'I'm so happy,' she said. 'I feel like a young girl again. Aunt Margaret, can we be married from here? I only have two weeks to arrange it all.'

'Two weeks!' Aunt Margaret looked shocked, then her eyes grew soft with memory as she recalled a young Geraldine telling her that she and Laurence couldn't wait. Geraldine would never change. She was still the same impulsive woman, full of the same joy and vitality which she had always possessed.

Eleanor travelled from Fairlaw and Terry managed to get forty-eight hours' leave before rejoining his squadron somewhere in the east of England.

'We're not allowed to give out information,' he told his family, and basked a little in the admiration of his mother and sisters, not to mention Aunt Margaret.

How delighted he was with his new family, thought Richard, when they all had a chance to get together before the wedding, though Eleanor had a whispered word for her mother.

'Have you told Alex Kinloch?' she asked.

Geraldine coloured a little. 'Certainly. At least, I . . . I've written to him,' she explained.

Nancy and Jonathan managed to join the family on the morning of the wedding. Nancy looked very glamorous in her favourite pastel green, contrasting with navy-blue for Eleanor who was her mother's bridesmaid. But Jonathan looked as untidy as ever in spite of Nancy's efforts to make him smart.

He looked tired, having newly returned from Suez where he had covered a news story on Sir Anthony Eden greeting the arrival of the first Australian and New Zealand troops.

Geraldine and Richard were married in Geraldine's old church near Lancaster Gardens. Her beauty and happiness were admired by everyone who saw her, but most of all by her new husband.

They had considered a honeymoon on board Richard's small motor launch, but in the end had decided to seek sanctuary in the peace and quietness of Richard's flat, which was now to become their home. It had changed little, Geraldine thought, as she wandered round the flat after removing her wedding clothes. She had put on a warm housecoat in pink wool trimmed with swans-down and she came to join Richard, who was relaxing in front of the fire.

'Tonight I don't have to part with you, my darling,' Richard told her, resting his chin on her hair. 'It was never easy for me to say good-night to you, Geraldine. I've always loved you.'

'It's wonderful to be so happy,' Geraldine told him.

Later, as she lay in his arms, she was conscious that her own passionate nature had not changed — she needed a man to love. She must never let Richard down, she vowed, as she kissed him and felt him stirring in his sleep.

* * *

Geraldine loved being back in London and she and Richard were ecstatically happy as she travelled around with him whilst he entertained the Forces, though occasionally he crossed to France to give performances to the troops stationed there. On these occasions Geraldine stayed with Aunt Margaret. She couldn't bear to be alone, dwelling on the shipping losses in the Channel and how vulnerable Richard was.

He was also inclined to be irritable when he returned from these trips and on one occasion when Geraldine had happily given him news of all her family and remembered, nostalgically, that she and Laurence had once been in exactly the same French towns as Richard had just visited, he turned on her.

'Must we talk all night about your family, Geraldine? I'm sure there must be other things happening in London. Haven't you seen any of our friends?'

163

Geraldine blinked, then warm colour began to burn in her cheeks. 'I understood that now we are married, you think of my family as being our family. I thought you'd want to hear about our family, and if by friends, you mean Eve Tarrant, then she's doing fine, thank you. She's off to America to make films about war-time Britain.'

Richard turned round slowly and stared at her. Geraldine's hair was untidy and her eyes were bright as diamonds. Suddenly he was laughing and holding out his arms.

'No-one can look madder than you, darling,' he told her. 'I'm sorry. It's just that you keep bringing Laurence into the conversation. It's as though he's still here . . . still claiming your love.'

'Of course he is. I can't pretend that I never had a previous husband. I've never had to shut him out of my life before . . . '

'No, but he was your only husband before. Now you have another one — me!'

164

'You're jealous!' Geraldine declared.

'Certainly I am. And you, my darling Geraldine, are jealous of my women friends, too. Why drag up Eve Tarrant? We haven't worked together for months.'

He sighed faintly. 'I'm sorry, Geraldine. I really do love my stepchildren and you know it.'

Geraldine stole a look at the lovely picture of Eve Tarrant in the paper and fought an urge to throw it in the waste-paper basket. But after a moment's hesitation, she put it down on a small table.

'Do you want to go out, or shall we have an early night?' Richard was asking.

Geraldine grinned.

'Oh, I think we'll just have an early night,' she said, and went into his arms.

★　★　★

Eleanor had returned to Hillcrest after her mother's wedding and had tried to settle down into the big old house which now seemed so empty despite the presence of the evacuees. One of them, a young woman, had returned to Glasgow with her small son, despite Eleanor's pleading for her to reconsider.

'The war's a long way from us, Miss Wyllie,' she told Eleanor. 'The Germans will only be bombing airfields, and naval bases and the like.'

'It's not over yet,' Eleanor said. 'I think we should all abide by what the authorities recommend.'

But the girl, whose new baby was due any time, decided to go home to be near the rest of her family in Glasgow and to take her small son with her.

'Good riddance,' Jenny Muir muttered. 'She wouldn't lift a finger to help and she aye got more than her share of the sugar. She was aye complaining.'

'I bet you've got the sugar rationed out to the last ounce.' Eleanor laughed, then her eyes grew serious. 'Can you spare a little if we have a guest for dinner on Sunday? Do you remember my friend, Paul Bryden, from Ayr? Well

. . . he's now in training at a naval station on the Forth. He's got thirty-six hours' leave, and I thought he could maybe come here since it's such a short leave.'

'I'll be delighted to see the young man, and don't you worry, Miss Eleanor, he'll not go short.' Jenny beamed. 'We've got our hens, and our own vegetables, which is more than a lot of folk.'

Eleanor nodded then went to prepare a room for Paul in case he could manage to stay. It was rather strange that they could write to one another with such ease, yet they found it difficult to talk to one another on the rare occasions when they met.

But it would be different this time, thought Eleanor, and for the first time she was glad that all her family would be away when Paul came. There would be no-one to inhibit the conversation. Her mother was so keen to do her best for everyone, but sometimes her enthusiasm was greater than her tact.

Eleanor paused a little, however, as she made up the bed in the guest room with snowy linen sheets. How she missed all of them; her mother, Terry, Nancy — her grandparents, too . . . How empty the house seemed. Yet how thankful she was to own the house. It represented such stability in her life, and it was still a home for all of them.

A point of view she later put to Paul Bryden.

'If you can stay overnight, Jenny and I will be delighted to entertain you,' she assured him. 'We're the only two left, except for one or two evacuees. One family has already gone back to Glasgow.'

'I believe that's happening in most cities.' Paul nodded. 'Don't you mind being in this big place by yourself?'

'No, of course not,' Eleanor said. 'It's my house now, you see. Grandfather left it to me in his will. He foresaw that I might be the only one still around here one day. Mother always wanted to go back to London and Nancy has already left home. And if Terry marries, his wife might want something different. But I love Hillcrest. It's my home.'

'I see,' Paul said, looking round the fine, well-proportioned drawing-room.

They had already eaten a wonderful dinner in the dining-room, a meal very different from the food he was at present eating every day. Now he viewed the lovely furniture, fine paintings and comfortable rugs with respect.

'I shall remember all this when I get back on duty,' he said ruefully.

'Surely I can offer you a proper bed for one night,' said Eleanor. 'The guest room is free. So is Terry's room, of course, if you'd prefer that.'

'No,' Paul said quickly, then softened his tone. 'No, I'm sorry, Eleanor, it's very kind of you and . . . and a great temptation to be in a real home again, even for a short while, but I . . . I must get back. There wouldn't be time.'

'There's a very early train from Fairlaw to Edinburgh,' she informed him.

'But I can't be sure of transport after Edinburgh and I'm on duty at midday. I must get back this evening, but ... well ... I'll never forget your kindness. It's been a great pleasure to see you again.'

Paul had gone, promising her he would write.

★   ★   ★

It had not occurred to Terry to go home to Fairlaw on a short leave. Normally he liked to spend his time in London, glad that he could now face his mother with pride. He was now an experienced pilot and expected promotion soon. He had flown with his squadron to attack air bases in Germany. He couldn't talk about such raids, but the knowledge that he had taken part and was now experienced in combat, gave him a new assurance.

Now, however, as Terry once again made the journey to London, he knew that this time he would not see his mother. He had been given careful instructions as to how to reach a Government office. He had been given no information as to why he was wanted, but he wasn't too worried. It could be no worse than some of the flak they had encountered over Germany.

The building was very unprepossessing and Terry checked the address before bounding up the stairs. Inside, however, a different atmosphere prevailed and a smart young woman in khaki uniform asked him to wait, then showed him through a door into a large office where two men sat behind a large desk.

A young girl sat in a chair facing them, and as she turned, Terry could hardly believe his eyes.

'Maria!' he cried. 'Maria! Is it really you?'

'Hello, Terry,' she replied, standing up as he walked forward and hugged her, then, in control of himself once more, he stood to attention as he realised that the two men were in uniform, one a major and the other a lieutenant-colonel.

'I . . . I apologise, sir,' Terry said awkwardly.

'Sit down, Wyllie.' The major indicated a seat and Terry sat down gingerly.

'You are well acquainted with Fraulein Maria Fischer,' the senior officer remarked, looking at the papers on his desk.

'Yes, sir,' Terry answered.

'In fact, you put yourself at some risk to get her out of Germany. Was this for any special reason other than the fact that you wished to marry her at that time?'

'At that time we do not wish to marry,' Maria put in. 'We do not marry now.'

Terry glanced at her.

'Maria felt that she could well be in danger if she remained in Germany,' he began. 'We saw what was happening to other people who shared her beliefs. I felt that I had to get her out.'

Swiftly he explained the circumstances, then a very detailed questioning began, during which Terry had to corroborate everything Maria had told them. He gave the names and addresses of all the people they had known and finally the senior officer nodded, satisfied.

'We have already checked most of this information, but we had to be sure that Maria Fischer could not remain in Germany for her own safety, and that she has no loyalty to the Nazi régime.'

'I still love my country,' Maria said proudly, 'but not the Nazis. I am ready to do whatever you say to help to take power from them and return that power to the real people of Germany.'

'That will be discussed later,' she was told. 'In the meantime we need not detain Pilot Officer Wyllie.'

Terry quickly leaped to his feet and Maria also rose, hoping to detain Terry for a while.

'Surely I can see my friend for a little while?' she asked.

The major nodded. 'He may wait for

you in the outer office. When are you due back on duty, Wyllie?'

'Twenty-three fifty-nine hours, sir.' He saluted smartly, then waited for Maria in the outer office. When she appeared, her face was radiant and together they descended the stairs.

'I cannot tell you it all, Terry,' she said, 'but I am out of jail.'

'Internment,' Terry corrected her.

'It is like jail. Now I make broadcast to the real Germans, people I know and love. Now I tell them the truth, not like Haw-Haw who tells us all lies. It is a good job, is it not?'

'A very good job,' Terry agreed. 'Oh, Maria, it's good to see you again. Why did you never write?'

'You know why,' she said. 'You would have wanted me back before you got used to doing without me. It is better that we stand on our own feet. You are a better man now, without me, and I am a better woman, without you. That is true, is it not? We can always be good friends, but we are not good for each other if we stay together.'

It was true. Their love had been too hot and passionate. It had seared them instead of supporting them. He still loved her, but in a different way, and she would always be his dear friend.

'Don't disappear out of my life again, though, will you?' he asked before they parted.

'No, I'll keep in touch,' she promised.

He kissed her, then ran for his train with a lightness of heart he had not felt for months. He need no longer worry about Maria.

⋆　⋆　⋆

Nancy had also been running for a train, though a different one. She had missed the last one and she knew that the few members of the orchestra who were performing with her would be waiting for her in Birmingham. Together they were doing a tour of works canteens before moving on to York, where they would entertain some of the troops. She was still doing occasional radio variety shows in London and she liked to come home as often as she could in the hope of seeing Jonathan.

When that happened, all the frustrations and longings of their many partings would vanish for a little while. Tiredly, Jonathan would thrust away his briefcase with all his papers and take Nancy in his arms and they would hold one another so closely that nothing else would matter.

Sometimes Nancy rebelled that they should be apart so much and coaxed Jonathan to try to remain in Britain, but Jonathan merely ruffled her fair curls.

'I have a job to do, Nancy. I don't have to search for news, but I never forget people are being killed.'

'Neither do I,' she flashed. 'Don't forget that I'm singing to some of those men. I get letters from them all the time.'

'Don't forget to wear your wedding ring.'

'That's a horrible thing to say!'

Soon they would be quarrelling,

each of them resenting the circumstances which forced them apart, and
each jealous of the other's career.
Often the words were meaningless and
not intended to hurt, but recently their
quarrels had been more serious,
thought Nancy, as she sat in the train
for Birmingham.

She had spent extra hours with
Jonathan and now she was late. This
had not happened since she first came
to London and started to sing with the
orchestra. She had lost her head then
and had gone out with young men to
parties and dances. In recent weeks she
had sometimes accepted such invitations again and had joined a party at a
hotel in the town where she was
performing.

Nancy had found herself laughing
and dancing with them as though she
were a young girl once more. Sometimes she had even wandered on to the
terrace of the hotel beside a man in
service uniform and had allowed him to
kiss her as a substitute for his girl back

in his own small town or village.

As Nancy Wyllie, singing to the Forces, she had felt she belonged to all of them, but always her private life had been very private, something which belonged only to her and Jonathan and not to be shared with anyone else. Now the dividing line had become blurred.

Uneasy And Anxious

The late spring had grown warm and suddenly the war news had become alarming. In early May, Germany invaded Holland, Belgium and Luxembourg, and Geraldine drew even closer to Richard as they listened each day to the news. Neville Chamberlain resigned as Prime Minister and Winston Churchill took his place.

In the early hours of Sunday, May 26, Richard received a telephone call from a friend living near Hastings and he woke Geraldine from a fitful and troubled sleep.

'I've got to go, darling,' he told her urgently. 'They're calling out all the small boats they can find to get our chaps off the beaches at Dunkirk. I've got my own motor launch, as you know — it was always my great love before the war — and it will carry a few fellows to safety.'

Geraldine was instantly awake. 'Wait! I'm coming with you!'

'No! There's not time. I've got to go,' Richard said huskily. 'It's no place for a woman.'

'I shall come as I am if you don't wait,' she told him.

Richard sighed. It was no use arguing with Geraldine when she was in this mood, and she might be able to help.

Later, Geraldine could only recall fragments of those terrible hours when men, many of them wounded, all of them wet, tired and hungry, were brought ashore in boatload after boatload. Richard worked tirelessly with his friend who looked after his boat, and Geraldine also helped, giving comfort where she could.

A short while later, Terry came home on leave and Richard insisted that he stay at the flat and set about making as much fuss of him as Geraldine. Terry had grown very tall and bore a remarkable resemblance to his father at the same age, and sometimes Geraldine caught a thoughtful look on Richard's face as he watched them.

However, for a little while he threw off his brooding expression and insisted on taking them all to one or two London shows and arranged a small dinner party for them. He included other young people in the party and Terry enjoyed himself thoroughly, though Geraldine thought she detected a feverishness in his enjoyment.

Later, when he was due to leave again for his base in the east of England, he held his mother tightly in his arms.

'Don't worry if I don't write for a few weeks,' he told her. 'We . . . we may be busy soon. Can't say more than that.'

She bit back the sudden tears and held him close.

'Oh, Terry!' she said. 'Take care, darling.'

'Don't worry, Mother. I'm pretty good at looking after myself.'

Geraldine watched him go and

Richard put his arms round her, comforting her.

All during that long hot summer she had lost weight as she listened avidly to news bulletins which told of the unbelievable heroism of the young men who intercepted German raids on air bases, in a mammoth struggle for air supremacy.

'They cannot invade or our Navy would sink all they've got,' Richard said, his eyes again holding their far-seeing look. 'They must gain supremacy in the air.' He fell silent.

'I can't bear it any longer, Geraldine,' he said at length. 'I've got to go. I can't stay at home while others take all the risks.'

She looked at him blankly. 'Go? Go where?'

'To join up, of course. The Navy. I know a great deal about the Navy and I've sailed my own boats both here and in America since I was in my early twenties. I would have something to give, Geraldine. I keep thinking about

Dunkirk . . . all those wounded men. And young men like Terry doing so much whilst I — '

'But you entertain the Forces! That's service!' Geraldine cried. 'That's a wonderful contribution.'

'I shall leave that to lovely young girls like Nancy and those more talented than I at making them forget the war for a little while. No, darling, it's not enough for me . . . '

The telephone shrilled, then shrilled again and Geraldine looked at it apprehensively. Richard's news had stunned her and for a moment she couldn't move. Pulling herself together, she picked up the receiver. A moment later she turned to look at Richard, the blood draining from her face.

'Who is it?' he asked. 'What's happened?'

Geraldine shook her head, listening intently.

'Oh, Anne,' she whispered. 'How dreadful. I'll come to see you and Philip straightaway.'

Slowly she replaced the receiver, crumpled into Richard's arms and burst into uncontrollable tears.

* * *

'It . . . it's Aunt Margaret,' she told him between sobs. 'You remember the Temples who lived next door to us at Lancaster Gardens — Philip and Anne Temple? Philip was Aunt Margaret's youngest brother.'

'I remember.' Richard nodded.

'They have a cottage in Suffolk and Aunt Margaret had gone to stay there for the weekend, but . . . but it's been hit by a stray bomb. I . . . I can't believe it . . . '

Richard held her tightly until her body stopped shuddering.

'Were Philip and Anne at the cottage?' he asked.

'They all were. It was only Aunt Margaret who was . . . was lost. Anne and Philip have cuts and bruises. They think it was a German plane which had jettisoned its bombs, but . . . but people were being evacuated into country areas for safety. It's so hard to understand, Richard.'

It was a gruelling week for Geraldine when once again she donned mourning clothes and attended Aunt Margaret's funeral.

Richard had been at her side, like a rock.

A few days later she learned that he had volunteered for service in the Royal Naval Volunteer Reserve and was waiting for his call-up papers. Geraldine was stunned.

'Oh, Richard, you can't mean it!' she cried. 'You can't just go and leave me like this.'

'It's not that I want to,' Richard said.

'You do! You must!' she said, unreasonably. 'Why are you volunteering? I'm going to be left with nobody.'

Geraldine knew she was behaving badly, but her emotions were in turmoil. The loss of Aunt Margaret had left her with a dull ache and all she

could look forward to each day was a
letter from Terry. Nancy was touring
the country with ENSA so that her
mother saw little of her and it was left
to Eleanor to telephone from time to
time. Alex Kinloch had now joined the
Royal Army Medical Corps and was
also somewhere in London.

Buckingham Palace was bombed and
the Royal Chapel wrecked, and soon
the whole of London seemed to
become, for Geraldine, one huge,
screaming noise — sirens, bombs,
gunfire, falling buildings, fire engines,
ambulances . . .

The noise roused Geraldine from her
apathy and she was galvanised into
action. She was deeply ashamed of her
own selfishness, and Richard couldn't
make her see that her behaviour had
just been a very normal reaction.

'No, I've done nothing to help
anybody, darling,' she said. 'I've done
nothing but feel sorry for myself. It will
be terrible to have to part with you, but
I know now why you have to go. And

186

now I must play my part, too. I've wasted so much time, Richard. I shall have to get in touch with someone and see where I would be most needed. Hospital work, perhaps, or WVS. Philip Temple has come out of retirement to do some sort of war work. Perhaps he can help me. At any rate, I must do something.'

'Don't worry, there's plenty of work for everyone,' Richard said.

He received his call-up papers a week or two afterwards and Geraldine clung to him, but Richard assured her that there would be a training period to be undertaken before he would be assigned to a ship on active service.

'I'll be home on leave in no time, darling,' he promised her, holding her close.

When he had gone, Geraldine rang Philip Temple who was doing work for the Civil Defence, and asked him to find her a job.

'I want to feel needed, Philip,' she told him. 'I know that Anne is with the

YWCA, but I thought something different might be for me. I want to be involved.'

'Let me think about it, Geraldine,' Philip suggested. 'I'll get back to you.'

★   ★   ★

A day or two later, Geraldine was caught up in a heavy raid, taking shelter in an underground station with countless others, and as she emerged, eventually, exhausted, hungry and thirsty, she mingled with bewildered people whose homes were damaged, people in need of food and shelter aimlessly wandering over the rubble which had once been their homes.

The local church hall near Geraldine's home had been annexed as a Rest Centre, and it was there that she started to work until Philip Temple found her something official.

Eleanor had telephoned her mother's flat several times and was very concerned when she received no reply, but happily Geraldine was in the flat one evening, when, for once, the sirens were mercifully quiet, and they managed to talk.

Eleanor was working equally hard at home, but there had been fewer sirens sounding in Fairlaw than in London. Some of her colleagues prophesied that Glasgow would soon be a target, but in the meantime Eleanor worried every day about her mother's safety.

She and Jenny Muir had listened to another broadcast Nancy had made, and Eleanor had tried to hide the tears which had sprung to her eyes. She had never been more lonely in her life, and she began to look forward, more and more, to Paul Bryden's regular letters, realising that she was deeply in love with him.

Knowing that soon he would be leaving on active service, Eleanor wrote inviting him to Hillcrest if he could again obtain a short leave: but there was no reply and Eleanor was in a quandary.

Should she have given Paul such a glimpse into her heart? Perhaps she had only succeeded in embarrassing him. Eleanor tried hard to come to terms with her own feelings, and Jenny Muir watched her silently, worried about how withdrawn the girl was becoming.

'It's time you had a day out,' she said bluntly. 'Or a holiday.'

'The school holidays aren't for weeks yet,' Eleanor pointed out.

'Go to Edinburgh on Saturday then,' Jenny argued. 'I need some new wool for knitting mufflers for the soldiers and they've run out at Armstrong's. Why don't you have a good dinner and go to the pictures?'

Eleanor allowed herself to be persuaded, and although she enjoyed her day out, it was nothing like the sort of outings she used to have with her mother and Nancy.

As she walked up the drive towards Hillcrest, she could see Jenny watching for her anxiously at the window. Eleanor's heart lurched, fearful that

Jenny had bad news for her, and she quickened her step to a run as Jenny came to open the door for her.

'What's wrong?' Eleanor panted.

'Did you see him at the station?' Jenny asked.

'Who?'

'The young sailor, Mr Bryden. He got time off to come looking for you and was very disappointed when you weren't here.'

Eleanor felt almost sick with disappointment. Her own train had passed the one bound for Edinburgh on the outskirts of Fairlaw.

'Why did I waste my time in Edinburgh?' she asked dismally. 'I can go there any time. Why couldn't he have let me know?'

'He had no time he said. He had to run for the train, but he says to tell you he'll write and not to worry if you don't hear for a wee while.'

The following day Eleanor received official notification that since her evacuees had now left Hillcrest, she was to be assessed for the billeting of Auxiliary Territorial Service officers, attached to the new anti-aircraft site on the outskirts of town.

A week later two young officers, Rosemary Archer of King's Lynn and Pamela Bishop of Stretford, moved into Hillcrest.

★   ★   ★

Towards the end of November, Nancy returned to London from the Midlands after carrying out a gruelling schedule of work. On the fourteenth of the month she had taken shelter as tons of bombs were dropped on Coventry, the devastation including the lovely old Cathedral, but for its spire.

Despite having learned to live with the bombs and to carry on singing and entertaining even as the anti-aircraft guns beat out their staccato rhythm, the bombing that night was so heavy that even Nancy was scared and for once, she joined her audience in one of the big communal shelters after her concert.

Her fears communicated themselves to a tall serviceman in khaki who had helped an elderly woman into the shelter. Having made the woman comfortable, he turned to smile at Nancy.

'I guess the noise is great in proportion to the amount of damage done, ma'am,' he drawled.

'I don't think so,' Nancy said shaking her head. 'There will be plenty of damage after this raid.'

'Maybe. Hope your home is not harmed.'

'My home is in London,' she told him. 'I've been here, working. I was due to take a train home, but I've missed it.'

'London has surely caught a packet as well.'

'Yes.' She looked at him more closely. 'You're American?'

'Canadian.' He grinned. 'I'm a rookie, as you would say. I have lived in the U.S. of A., but the past few years

I've settled in Hamilton, Ontario.'

'And I was born in London, but have lived nearly all my life in Fairlaw, near Edinburgh.'

'Lovely city. I went there on a short leave, also to Hamilton, Scotland.'

Nancy found herself responding to his friendly grin.

'If you're nervous, sing a little song,' the Canadian soldier suggested.

She stared. 'Have I sung for you at the Forces concert? I mean, did you know that I'm a singer?'

'No, I was cheering you up, but if you can sing, ma'am, then let us all hear. I'll play my mouth-organ.'

Nancy had never felt like singing, but as the soldier began to play a popular number, she began to sing and soon everyone was joining in. She sang one of her own favourites. 'Wishing Will Make It So' and saw that many people had tears in their eyes.

'You surely are a nightingale,' the man told her. 'By the way, my name is

Greg — wait for it — Greg Hamilton!'
he told her.

They laughed together.

'Nancy Duke,' she said. 'Nancy
Wyllie when I'm singing.'

'I'd sure like to see you again,
Nancy.'

'Maybe sometime,' she agreed. 'I've got
to get back to London now.' Impulsively
she searched in her handbag for an old
envelope. 'Here's my address in London.
That's my husband's name. He's a war
correspondent. If you have no friends in
England, perhaps I could find someone
for you to contact. It must be lonely to
be so far from home.'

'I would settle for Nancy Wyllie.'
He grinned and again they laughed
together. When the all-clear sounded,
Nancy was glad to have Greg Hamilton
to escort her from the shelter. The
devastation was so awful that she could
hardly bear to look at it.

In London, she found that the
windows of the flat had been blown in,
but very little other damage had been

done. Letters from Jonathan were waiting for Nancy but she gained no comfort from them. They were merely pieces of paper when she wanted the warmth and comfort of Jonathan's love to help her fight the fatigue which was beginning to pursue her these days.

Nancy stuck up the windows with cardboard and brown paper, then crawled into bed.

How lonely the flat seemed when she was by herself.

She had been very lonely recently, though she had liked talking to Greg Hamilton.

He was an interesting man, Nancy decided. He had promised to spend his next forty-eight-hour pass in London. It might be rather nice to see him again.

Geraldine was finding plenty to do in her unofficial job whilst waiting for something to come up from Philip Temple.

One dark winter's night in January of 1941 she found Terry waiting for her outside the flat. Geraldine's heart bounded with delight when she saw him. It was some weeks since she had heard from Richard who had now joined his ship as a Lieutenant, and Terry's letters had been few and far between.

With every news bulletin full of the number of aircraft being shot down Geraldine lived in a constant state of tension and fear that something had happened to her son.

'Darling, you should have let me know you were coming,' she told him. 'I don't know what's in the food cupboard.'

'I rang you several times,' Terry told her, 'but there was no reply. I can't tell you I'm coming if you're not here.' There was a touch of asperity in his tone and Geraldine looked at her son closely. His face was quite thin and gaunt and there was a nervous tic at the side of his eye. He looked very tired.

'You need looking after,' she said, after she had found him a snack. 'But I must help while I can. People are beginning to depend on us at the centre. Terry, why don't you go home to

Fairlaw for a few days?'

'Because I wanted to see you, and I thought you might want to see me,' he said, and immediately Geraldine rushed to assure him that she did want to see him.

'How could you think otherwise!' she cried. 'I'm only thinking about you. The worst raids are slackening off a little, but you need rest.'

'Hold on.' He grinned and some of the old mischief was in his eyes. 'I'm only teasing you a bit. As a matter of fact, I'm here for another purpose as well. I'm taking Maria out tomorrow night. We might do a show if we can find one which hasn't been bombed out. Would you like to come, too, as a change from listening to Tommy Handley in 'Itma'?'

Slowly she shook her head.

'I really can't, but I'm glad you're seeing Maria. She's doing propaganda work, isn't she? Terry, are you and she . . . ?'

'Nosy Parker,' he said, lightly pushing

at the tip of her nose. 'Wouldn't you like to know? Oh, all right, I won't tease you any more. No, we're good friends, but that's all now.'

'I'm glad,' Geraldine sighed. 'Though I'm fond of her, too.'

Terry stayed in London for a few more days, then decided to take his mother's advice and move to Fairlaw.

Eleanor was delighted to hear from him when he telephoned, and said she would have his room all ready for him.

'There's just one thing, Terry,' she said hesitantly.

'What?'

'Oh . . . nothing, really.' The line grew crackly. 'I'll be looking out for you, Terry. Will you only manage to stay for a week?'

'I'm lucky to have that,' he told her. 'I've used up part of my leave already.' His eyes were thoughtful as he hung up the receiver.

Geraldine was glad for Terry, but sorry for herself after he had left for Scotland. The few days he had spent at the flat only served to emphasize its emptiness now that Richard had gone. Sometimes Geraldine felt that she couldn't bear it a moment longer.

Nancy had come to see her, dressed in her smart khaki uniform with ENSA at the top of each sleeve, and although she could well understand Nancy's loneliness when Jonathan was away, she also felt uneasy and anxious for her younger daughter.

'I would feel better if Jonathan were in the forces, then at least I would know where he was.' Nancy had told her. 'But sometimes he's in Crete, then he's in the Sudan, and I'm sure he's in constant danger. I can't live like this, worrying about him all the time. My . . . our . . . youth is being wasted.'

Geraldine listened to the correction, but she knew that Nancy really was thinking about her own youth.

'Try to be patient, darling,' she urged. 'He really is worth it.'

Accusations

Geraldine was thinking about Richard as she climbed the stairs a day or two after Terry had left. She hardly noticed that the light was on in the flat, and the blackout already drawn, until she had opened the door and wearily closed it again.

Then as she walked into the large drawing-room, Richard's tall figure rose from his favourite seat, and he held out his arms to his wife. With a small cry Geraldine stumbled towards him and was enfolded in her husband's arms.

'No going down into the shelter for us tonight,' she said, after they had caught and held each other, their kisses searing as they clung together. 'I refuse to share a moment of our time together with anyone else in this world. I just want to stay in your arms, darling. The bombs can do their worst tonight.'

Richard's smile was warm and his kisses passionate, as he thanked God for the love and tenderness of this wonderful woman.

It was very late when Terry reached Fairlaw. The train had been crowded with many young service people sitting in the corridors on their kitbags. It had been held up on more than one occasion, and although Eleanor had waited up for her brother, he wanted nothing more than his own bed when he finally arrived at Hillcrest.

'We can't make a noise,' Eleanor whispered, 'because of — '

'I'm too tired to do anything but snore,' Terry told her wearily. 'I'll see you in the morning, Eleanor.'

He hugged her quickly and disappeared into his room.

Eleanor padded quietly to her own room, hoping that Terry remembered that she had the ATS officers, Subaltern Rosemary Archer and Second Subaltern Pamela Bishop billeted at Hillcrest. The girls would be asleep by now, but by the look of Terry, he wasn't likely to be parading the corridors this night.

Terry had a good refreshing sleep, but woke up feeling sticky and travel stained from the previous evening. For a moment he lay looking round his old bedroom, relishing the thought that he was home, then he leaped out of bed. It was warm enough to do without his dressing-gown but he collected his shaving kit and walked barefooted along to the bathroom, throwing open the door with a feeling of well-being and energy.

There was a girl in the bath!

For an eternity they stared at one another, then the girl gave a small screech and the soap suds seemed to leap up in a frenzy as she tried to hide underneath them.

Terry was conscious of his own scanty coverings and quickly excused himself. He remembered now his mother telling him that two ATS officers had been billeted at Hillcrest. Well, it served the girl right for not locking the door!

Terry put this point of view to Eleanor when he arrived downstairs in the breakfast-room.

'The lock's broken,' Eleanor told him. 'We've got a time system going. Pamela had the bathroom at seven, and Rosemary at seven-thirty this week. I was going to tell you last night, but you were so tired I thought you would sleep in.'

They could hear the girls talking as they came downstairs and, as they came into the breakfast-room, Terry rose to his feet.

'This is my brother, Terence,' Eleanor said. 'Miss Rosemary Archer, Miss Pamela Bishop . . . '

'We'd better skip the porridge this morning, if Jenny doesn't mind,' Pamela said. 'We're late.'

Terry was running an expert eye over the two girls. The shorter of the two, Pamela Bishop, was a blonde with mischievous brown eyes and a wide smile. The other girl was tall with smooth, dark hair, delicate apple-blossom complexion and blue eyes which were at the moment shooting electric sparks in his direction. He grinned a little and tried to put them at their ease, as Eleanor hurried out of the room to give Jenny her instructions for the day.

'I doubt if you'll miss having a Jerry plane in your sights if you eat a plate of porridge,' he said easily. 'Best have a good breakfast or you might shoot down one of our chaps by mistake.'

It had been the wrong thing to say. Rosemary's embarrassment was turning to anger.

'We are highly trained for our job, Wing Commander,' she said icily, 'and we are certainly not allowed to be late on duty.'

Terry looked at Pamela who was doing her best to control a grin.

'Of course you mustn't be late on duty,' he agreed, 'but you'll work all that much better if you relax and be friendly. I mean . . . we can't exactly be strangers, can we? We accomplished quite a good introduction very quickly . . . '

Rosemary stared at him frostily, then looked at her watch.

'Come on, Bishop,' she said clearly. 'We've no time to waste.'

They were leaving the house as Eleanor returned to the breakfast-room, dressed ready for school.

'Oh . . . the girls have gone,' she said surprised.

'I'm the culprit,' Terry admitted. 'Sub Archer thinks I am a bad smell.'

'Oh, Terry! You've probably embarrassed her. Anyway, I've got to go now. What are you doing today?'

'Mending the lock on the bathroom door.' Terry smiled.

★　★　★

Nancy was longing for a letter — from Jonathan. Sometimes, though, no news was good news in his case. It could mean he was on his way home from some assignment and would shortly turn up at the flat, and this time he would find her at home.

So often she was away on tour while he was home, but Nancy had been booked to make a series of broadcasts on the Forces network and, she hoped, would be able to remain in London for a few weeks. Delighted as she was to be doing the broadcasts, she found it frustrating that there was no Jonathan to share the excitement with her.

Nancy was about to let herself into the flat one evening when a tall man in khaki stepped forward to meet her.

'Remember me?' he asked. 'You said I could come to see you, Miss Nancy Wyllie, and I'm surely doing just that, if only to tell you I've heard you singing on the radio and I'm a fan.'

She stared at him for a long moment, then she laughed.

'I hadn't forgotten you,' she assured him. 'Your name is . . . '

'Hamilton!' they chorused.

'Call me Greg,' he invited.

'Greg,' she agreed. 'Come on in. I'm

just back from the studios, as a matter of fact. We've been hard at it all day, but I think the programme will be quite a success. I've also been recording, 'Remember Me By Moonlight'.'

'I surely will!' Greg said admiringly as the full moon brought brightness to the night sky and Nancy's lovely delicate face looked back at him, enchantingly, as she opened the door of her flat.

'I'll do the black-outs,' he offered. 'I'm a dab hand.'

'Do you miss your home, your wife?' she asked with sympathy.

'My home, yes. No wife — yet. But I have a nice girl waiting for me when all this is over. She's a bit like you, Nancy Wyllie, but she can't sing a note. Wait till I tell her about you and take back your records. You'll have to sign them for me.'

'Delighted!' Nancy laughed. 'I can now claim one fan.'

'I'll represent all of them,' Greg said generously. 'If you're tired, Nancy, and you don't mind a man in your kitchen, I'll fix you a bite of food. It's a pleasure to be in a real home again.'

Nancy relaxed, thinking this was what Jonathan did sometimes when they spent a quiet evening together.

She enjoyed her spam and salad, washed down with a glass of wine, which Greg had also found in the cupboard. He told her about his family in Canada: his parents, brothers and sisters, and the girl he had known all of his life.

In return she told him about her own family and how much she missed Jonathan when he was away.

'Do you think he would object if I asked you out tomorrow night, Nancy?' Greg asked. 'Here am I eating all your rations. I guess it's only fitting if I take you to eat in a nice restaurant, even if they only serve 'bangers'.'

'I'd love to have a night out.' Nancy smiled.

She felt a twinge of guilt when she thought about Jonathan, and the dangers he might be facing while she was out enjoying herself, but she dismissed these thoughts. Jonathan would understand that she deserved a little fun now and then.

★   ★   ★

The authorities were better organised now, and Geraldine had less to do at the centre. One or two other women were now helping out and she found herself with more time on her hands.

The flat was lonely when Richard was away and Geraldine had spent some time at her 'Make Do And Mend' tasks, mainly making patchwork cushions and bedspreads so that the flat would seem more like home to her than merely Richard's flat.

Anne Temple had offered her Aunt Margaret's lovely antique work-box as a remembrance of the old lady and Geraldine offered to collect it from Lancaster Gardens.

'Come and have tea tomorrow,' Anne

invited. 'Philip wants to talk to you, anyway, about a job.'

'What sort of job?' Geraldine asked excitedly. 'I'd love something really worthwhile.'

'I gather this would be worthwhile,' Anne said cagily, 'but I really don't know any more than that.'

A few days later, Geraldine found herself, dressed in her most business-like suit, being led along endless corridors under the War Office by a young woman in uniform. She was shown into a small room where an equally young lieutenant rose to greet her. Carefully he took down her name, address and age.

'I understand you're interested in photography, Mrs Ransome?'

'I've only done it as a hobby,' Geraldine told him. 'My mother-in-law loved photographs and kept fine albums. I carried it on after she died, but I liked to take my own photographs.'

'You have a keen eye?'

'I don't really know.'

'You would have to be observant. Training would be given, of course. Now could you look at these aerial photographs and see if you can recognise any of them? Also, if I show you two of the same area, can you compare them and see if anything has been added or taken away.'

The aerial photographs were different from anything Geraldine had ever seen, but soon she found herself becoming absorbed in what she was asked to do. Some of the photographs were of parts of London she knew, though it took her some minutes to recognise them. Comparing two photographs was even more absorbing, and she was quick to spot any differences in them.

The young lieutenant thanked her gravely and asked her to wait. Eventually another, more senior, officer came to interview her and to explain fully what she would be required to do if her tests proved successful. She would receive official notification about all that in due course.

Geraldine went home feeling excited, yet unsettled. She had no doubt at all that the work she might be asked to do was important war work. But was it what she wanted? She wished Richard was here to discuss these problems with her, but he wasn't, and she knew it must be her own decision.

★　★　★

Terry enjoyed his leave. Not only was it wonderful to be home even for a short while, but to have the entertaining presence of Rosemary Archer and Pamela Bishop to keep any boredom away was a great bonus. Not that he was making much headway with Rosemary, and had it not been for the fact that he had stood watching her from the concealment of his bedroom window curtain one day, he would have dismissed her as a rather stand-offish girl with a very dull personality.

On their day off, the girls had

retrieved two old deck-chairs from an outhouse and had braved the rather chilly winds to enjoy a little bit of pale sunshine in the garden.

Terry watched them talking together, though he was too far away to overhear any conversation, but he was struck by the animation on Rosemary's face as she turned to smile at her friend.

Her hair had come loose from the neat roll which she wore under her cap in order to keep it two inches above the collar, and a faint breeze blew tendrils of it against her cheek. It was such a pity, thought Terry, that she kept him at arm's length. She obviously couldn't forget that they'd got off to a bad start and whereas Terry often thought it was hilarious and couldn't help teasing her accordingly, Rosemary had never been prepared to see the joke.

Terry had turned his attention on Pamela, who was much more his type. She loved fun and dancing, and was full of the joy of living, but he had learned straightaway that she was already engaged to a young man who was serving with the Military Police.

'He's a Redcap,' she told Terry. 'Bob and I grew up together. He's going into the police service after the war, if he can.'

'Where did you grow up together?' Terry asked.

'Stretford, near Manchester. Rosemary is from King's Lynn. Don't tease her so much, Terry. She's a very shy, sensitive person.'

'I'll take your word for it,' Terry told her ruefully. He had offered to take both girls dancing, but Rosemary had turned down that idea. Now Terry did not see why Pamela couldn't come on her own Rosemary could keep Eleanor company for just one evening.

'I don't suppose Bob would mind,' Pamela said, after a bit of thought. 'He's in Aldershot at the moment. OK, Terry, let's go.'

Terry had a wonderful evening. Pamela had boundless energy and could match his steps perfectly so that they danced every dance. She was completely natural with him and a wonderful companion. They were still singing some of the catchy dance tunes when they returned home.

'Would Bob mind if I kissed you good-night?' Terry asked as they walked arm in arm down the drive.

'As long as he doesn't know about it,' Pamela grinned, reaching up to give him a quick kiss. 'I don't believe in rushing off to tell him that I've enjoyed someone else's company, merely to clear my own conscience. Nor, for that matter, do I want to know what he's up to. We're both young and neither of us cares to live a very dull life. It might make us dull people.'

Terry looked down at her small merry face in the pale moonlight of the spring evening.

'Suddenly I'm sorry you're engaged,' he said.

'None of that! We've had a good time, and that's all. I am engaged to Bob. We're right for each other and we'll have a good marriage after the war.'

'You're a nice girl, Pam,' Terry told her. 'I don't see why I can't kiss you again.'

'I saw you,' Rosemary accused her after Pamela tiptoed up to the bedroom which had once been Geraldine's. 'You let him kiss you. What would Bob say?'

'He'd tell me to behave myself, which I have done. Terry Wyllie is no angel, but he's a gentleman. Why don't you give him a chance to get to know you, Rosie? You're well named when I call you Rosie. You're beautiful enough, but you've grown a few thorns. And all because he's seen you in the altogether.'

'He did not! I was under the suds.'

Pamela giggled and a pillow hit her on the back of the neck.

'He's a wolf,' Rosemary said. 'I know his type.'

'Give him a chance, Rosie. If you don't, I shall have to go out with him again, then Bob will like it even less. I might be tempted to kiss Terry three times!'

'Oh . . . you!' Rosemary said, exasperated.

* * *

Nancy was receiving more and more fan letters and Greg Hamilton was pleased and proud to help her sort them out. He was still with his unit in London, but his spell of training would soon be at an end and Greg knew that he would soon be going overseas.

He and Nancy had become great friends over the past few weeks and together they had managed to do all the small jobs needed in the flat. The windows had been replaced, and Greg had repaired cracks and made her kitchen shelves more secure.

He took such pleasure in the work that Nancy had no compunction in finding all the tasks for him which were waiting to be done. Now he helped her to sort out her fan mail, and seemed to enjoy it as much as she did herself.

He was on his knees on the floor as

they sorted out the letters, and suddenly she was aware of his scrutiny and turned to stare at him. For a long time he looked deeply into Nancy's eyes, then suddenly she was in his arms and he was kissing her passionately.

'Oh, Nancy, honey,' he whispered. 'I didn't see it coming. I should have. I'm a great fool, but I've fallen in love with you.'

'Greg.' She whispered his name, and again he took her in his arms and she closed her eyes . . .

Greg was stroking her hair and pulling her into his arms and again she felt the strength of his lips on her own, and for a long moment she just wanted to remain in his arms. Then she pushed him away and scrambled to her feet.

'It's late, Greg, later than usual. You'll really have to go.'

'Sure.' He was buttoning on his tunic. 'I can't leave it like this, honey. I guess I've never felt this way about a girl before.'

'Oh, Greg!' Nancy was close to tears.

She didn't know how she felt. She only knew that she hadn't felt this way since . . . since her marriage. She was married to Jonathan, but it seemed a long time since she had been in Jonathan's arms.

Jonathan came home two days later and he immediately knew that there had been another man in the flat. There was no-one at home when he let himself in with his key, but the smell of tobacco seemed to hang around the flat and the door no longer creaked when he opened it. The lock had been oiled. Jonathan had always refused to oil it. He liked the sound it made when he opened his own front door.

Inside the flat he found that the new windows had been painted and that the kitchen sink had new tiles surrounding it so that it could be wiped easily. The cupboard door was firmly fixed in place and a jar of peanut butter, half finished, stood on the shelf. Nancy hated peanut butter.

She came home, tired but in a

strange state of euphoria, two hours later and the sudden widening of her eyes when she saw him cut Jonathan to the heart. Always Nancy had rushed into his arms, but this time his welcome from her was a great deal more restrained.

'Hello, darling,' she said simply. 'Have you had something to eat? Just let me drop this bag of shopping and I'll find you something. I've got to empty it, though. They don't wrap things up these days.'

'I've had a peanut butter sandwich,' he told her, and she whirled round, and they stared at each other for what seemed like an eternity.

'Who is he?' he asked.

'Nothing's happened, Jonathan. I — '

'Who is he?'

'A friend. He's a Canadian soldier . . . Greg Hamilton.'

'Is he in love with you?'

Her face told him the answer to that.

'You're always away so long,' she said painfully. 'He's just a friend, Jonathan.

He helped me do jobs in the house.'

He made a snorting sound and suddenly she was angry.

'All right, they were your jobs in *your* house, but where were you? Do you have to be away so much?'

'Most men of my age in this country have to be away from home,' he told her harshly. 'If they're married men, they expect to find their wives waiting for them. It's no harder than having to go out and fight. But I had to marry 'The Girl They Left Behind'. I had to marry the girl who belongs to thousands of men.' His voice changed. 'I didn't mind the thousands, Nancy, but one is one too many.'

Her face was very white, her eyes enormous. 'I told you nothing has happened, but now I don't care what you think. I'm not staying here to have you throw insults at me.'

She whirled round and rushed out of the flat, hardly knowing how she managed to reach Geraldine's flat. Her one desire was to rush to her mother to tell her what had happened, to seek reassurance that she had done no wrong. It was Jonathan who was unfair, Jonathan who didn't understand.

The flat was in darkness. Nancy didn't know that Geraldine had now started doing very special war work. Slowly she turned away and went back home. She would have to talk to Jonathan again, but when she returned, she found the flat empty. It was as though Jonathan had never been there.

Prolonged Partings

Geraldine began to be absorbed in her new job and as the cold winter days gave way to warm spring weather, her spirits rose accordingly. In early May, Richard came home on leave and they listened together to the news that Rudolf Hess had parachuted into Scotland.

'That's marvellous news, isn't it, darling?' Geraldine asked eagerly. 'Surely it must mean something. Perhaps Hitler wants to finish the war.'

'You are an optimist,' Richard said, shaking his head. 'If Hitler had parachuted down along with Hess, I might give it more credence, but it merely suggests to me that Hess has gone crazy.'

'Pessimist!' Geraldine retorted.

She went to answer the telephone. It was Eleanor, and Richard sighed. No doubt they would talk for hours and he'd wanted to take Geraldine out for a break. It was time they had a little fun.

But when Geraldine came back, her face was very white and her eyes full of distress.

'It's bad news, Richard,' she said. 'Alex Kinloch. His house-keeper sent a message to Eleanor. Alex has been killed. He has been working at a hospital in Liverpool.'

Richard held her closely, but for once Geraldine could not find comfort in tears. Alex had taken the news of her marriage well and had wished her every happiness, but often she'd wanted to see him again. Now it was too late . . .

Eleanor, too, found the news about Alex Kinloch very upsetting. It was as though she were losing all the people she had known and loved when she was a child. Rosemary and Pamela were now good friends of hers, but their heavy spells of duty meant that they were out in the evenings while she was alone at home.

On the Saturday following her phone

call to her mother regarding Alex, she was helping Jenny with the housework when she looked out of the window, her attention caught by someone walking up the drive. Seconds later Eleanor rushed to the front door, oblivious of the fact that she was wearing one of Jenny's voluminous overalls. She saw Paul Bryden breaking into a run, too, and she held out her arms as she rushed towards him.

'Oh, Paul! I'm so glad to see you,' she said. 'I'm so glad you've come.' She reached up to kiss him, but suddenly she was aware of the interested gaze of old Matthew Craig, who delivered their milk.

'You've got your young man here, I see, Miss Eleanor,' he remarked. 'Och, but it's good to see the lad's home on leave.'

Eleanor blushed self-consciously, realising how ridiculous she must look in Jenny's flowered overall.

'Come on in, Paul,' she said, laughing. 'Jenny will have the kettle on for Matthew here. I expect we'll all enjoy a cup of tea.'

Paul was glad to follow her into the house.

'How long have you got?' she asked after she had removed the apron. 'Can you stay overnight, Paul?'

'Not this time. I've only got today and I have to be back at twenty-two hundred hours. I won't even manage home to see my father. He's in the house by himself now, since we lost my mother.'

'I was so sorry to hear about your mother. Paul,' Eleanor said with warm sympathy.

'Father may want to give up the house and go to stay with my aunt. It's a rented house, you see. That would mean I'd have to make my own way . . . build up my own home . . . after the war.'

'Your job in the bank will be waiting for you,' Eleanor pointed out. 'It isn't going to be the same as after the First World War when many servicemen came home to find their jobs taken by others.'

'I know, but . . . '

★   ★   ★

'Here's the tea now, Miss Eleanor,' Jenny said, coming in with a tray. 'Should I get extra eggs from Matt Craig? Our hens have gone off their lay just now. I think they're on the moult.'

'Certainly. Yes, of course, Jenny,' Eleanor said vaguely.

The house was always too busy for holding a private conversation with anyone, she thought, as she heard the front door opening and the bright voices of Rosemary and Pamela in the hall.

'Our ATS officers,' she explained to Paul.

'Oh, yes?' He looked at her as though he would like to say more, but again the door opened and the girls walked in, greeting them cheerfully. Soon there was a great deal of laughter and happy banter as the girls produced a few delicacies bought from their canteen, and Eleanor poured out cups of tea.

'I'll try to get another pass,' Paul told Eleanor when it was time to go. 'We've still got a lot to do in the war before we can think too far ahead.'

Geraldine had to get up early to be on duty each day, and sometimes she was late in arriving home. Hitherto she had found this satisfying and even stimulating. Her fatigue from working long hours had been tempered by deep inner satisfaction that she was doing something worth while.

It was easy to catch up on the household tasks when there was only herself in the flat, but when Richard came home on leave everything changed. He didn't want to part with her all day and every day, even though he appreciated that she had no choice but to stick to her duties.

At first he was tired and appreciated the quiet peace of the flat, then he began to look up old friends.

'I've asked a few people round tomorrow night, darling,' he told Geraldine. 'Can you be early for once?'

She had kicked off her shoes and was sitting in her favourite chair by the fireside.

'Have a rest then we'll go out for dinner,' he suggested.

She shook her head, her eyes tired. 'No, I've been poring over photographs all day. My head aches, Richard. Can you put up with something on a tray?'

'We had something on a tray last night. This is my leave, Geraldine. I'm back on duty in two days. At least we can have some fun tomorrow night.'

'I'll have a job providing food for a party.'

'Don't you worry about that,' he assured her. 'I'll attend to it. This flat has seen many a gathering in the old days before — '

He broke off and she finished the sentence.

'Before you married a tired old lady.'

'Before I married the woman I love,' he corrected her.

Geraldine sighed and tried hard to respond to his mood. She would have to try to be home early the following evening. This leave was not much fun for Richard. He was full of enthusiasm, and he kept up his dance routines every day, and practised new songs. She had no doubt he entertained his fellow officers when they were off duty.

He hardly aged, she thought, as she watched him walking around the flat with his quick, youthful step.

The following evening the party was in full swing when Geraldine arrived home, and she tried to be bright as she greeted their guests, then quickly made her way to the bedroom to freshen up and change her dress.

She had felt old ever since . . . ever since she heard the sad news about Alex Kinloch, she realised. His death had fallen like a heavy cloak about her shoulders and, when she thought about the many years they had been friends, she had grown more and more conscious of the passing time.

Now she didn't feel ready to be bright and happy for Richard's friends. How dull they must think her! She felt dull, she who had never before felt dull in the whole of her life. Even her pretty dress in her favourite shade of deep red seemed too young for her.

'Ready, darling?' Richard's voice asked behind her. 'No need to worry about food. The guests have all brought something along. Everyone seems to do that these days.'

It seemed hours before they all went, and Geraldine's head ached with the effort of appearing bright and amusing.

'Leave everything and I'll tidy it up in the morning,' she said to Richard after the last guest had gone. 'I only want to go to bed.'

'Good idea,' Richard said happily.

She lay in bed feeling that every bone in her body was aching. They were old bones, she decided forlornly. She was no longer a young girl. Even when

Richard leaped into bed and pulled her towards him, happy to relax after the fun evening, Geraldine found she had no response to offer him.

'I'm so tired, Richard,' she said. 'I have to be on duty in the morning.'

He said nothing but she could sense his disappointment in her. She was too tired to even worry about that disappointment.

★   ★   ★

Terry was looking forward to his next leave. He had now clocked up many hours' flying time, and more and more he was being given heavy responsibility for the planning of operations and the training of new young pilots. He found this more nerve-racking than the actual flying and he was always glad to step off the train at Fairlaw to begin ten days' leave.

The anti-aircraft battery on the outskirts of the town had grown in size and there were many more Service people walking the streets. Happily, Pamela Bishop and Rosemary Archer, now a Junior Commander, were still billeted at Hillcrest, and Pamela greeted Terry with delight.

'We have dancing every Saturday night in our camp now,' she told him. ''In The Mood' . . . Joe Loss and his Band. We play records, you know. We must try out a few new steps, Terry. Can you jitter-bug?'

'But of course.' He grinned. 'Sounds great, Pam.'

'Rosemary doesn't do much dancing but she's helping to organise a play. Tell him about it, Rosie.'

Rosemary flushed. She still felt awkward with Terry Wyllie. He had the habit of staring at her intently so that she felt awkward and embarrassed.

'I hardly think the Wing Commander would be interested,' she said quietly.

'Oh, but I would!' Terry assured her.

'Rosemary is gathering all the props together,' Pamela told Terry, with an engaging grin. 'I don't suppose you have an old rocking horse in the attic?'

'As a matter of fact, I have,' Terry said.

Rosemary stared at him, her eyes widening.

'Have you really?' she asked.

'In the attic,' he assured her. 'Mind you, it's some years since it was used. It will need to be cleaned up.'

'I don't mind that,' she said quickly.

A large screw was broken, but Terry had found one almost as big, and in conjunction with the glue pot it seemed to hold the rocker together quite well. He worked on it happily during the day and occasionally Eleanor popped her head round the door of the shed and offered words of encouragement. He had borrowed the radio and listened avidly to the news as he worked.

In June, Germany had attacked Russia and the news was long and detailed as it dealt with every front of the war.

'I wouldn't like to be some of the Navy chaps,' Terry told Eleanor, 'having to get supplies of armaments to Russia. That's what they are going to need, you'll see. You've got to hand it to those men, though.'

Eleanor shivered, but said nothing. Paul was back at sea, but she had no idea where he was at the moment.

'Mind your skirt on that paint!' Terry warned her, but it was too late. A streak of black paint had been slashed across the brown tweed of Eleanor's skirt as she brushed against the paintbrush.

'Oh, Terry!' she cried. 'You careless twit! Why did you have to leave it there?'

Terry blinked. It was rare for his sister to lose her temper.

'I'm leaving it all to dry,' he told her. 'Then I'll put it up into the old play-room. Rosemary doesn't want it just yet. Sorry, Eleanor. I'll clean that skirt up for you, if you like.'

'No fear,' said Eleanor. 'I'll see what I can do with it myself.'

Terry was proud of his efforts.

'It's perfect,' he said proudly. 'Good

as new and in time for the dress rehearsal!'

* * *

But was it, he wondered, as he lay in bed that night. The glue should be well set by now but that screw had not been quite the right size. The horse had to be ridden by a boy in the play, and the boy was being played by one of the ATS girls. Suppose the horse came apart right there in front of the audience — Rosemary would be so embarrassed.

Terry couldn't settle until he'd tried out the horse for himself. If it bore his weight, then it would be strong enough for a slim girl. Softly he padded into the old nursery and climbed up on top of the horse, then began to sway gently backwards and forwards.

Rosemary heard the rhythmic squeaking noise through the wall of her bedroom, having been startled out of her sleep, and for once she was sorry that Pamela, who snored a little, was away for the weekend. Someone had broken in and was sawing as quietly as possible at a locked cupboard or drawer. Without troubling to put on her dressing-gown or slippers, she quietly opened the door, then stealthily pushed open the door of the next room.

The light was blazing and Terry, who had been standing on the stirrups to test them, turned with a startled cry as the horse wobbled under him. A moment later he lost his balance and fell to the floor, turning his ankle on the strong wooden base of the horse.

He gave a small moan of pain as Rosemary ran forward and helped him to his feet.

'I was only testing the beastly thing,' he said crossly. 'Now I've twisted my ankle.'

'I'll have to help you back to your bedroom,' Rosemary said. 'Can you lean on me? I'll strap it up for you. There's a first-aid kit in the bathroom — quietly now,' she whispered, as she helped him to hobble to his bedroom across the hall.

Rosemary was very quick and deft, and soon the ankle had been treated with cold compresses, and was now strapped up in a competent fashion.

'You'll need to see the doctor in the morning,' she said. 'It's quite a bad sprain.'

'I expect I will,' he said dolefully. 'I won't be able to go back off leave like this. I'll have to let my C.O. know. How can I explain that I sprained my ankle falling off a rocking horse in the middle of the night?'

His cheeks had flushed with embarrassment and there was misery in his eyes, but suddenly Rosemary found that laughter was beginning to bubble inside her. She tried to stifle it, but the situation seemed to grow increasingly funny, and her laughter exploded so that she sat on the floor and rocked herself helplessly.

'What's so funny?' Terry demanded, scowling. 'You have no idea how embarrassed I feel.'

'Oh, but it's so funny,' Rosemary

said. 'Oh, I'm aching all over. Here you are, living a charmed life, flying on countless missions without a scratch, and now you've injured yourself falling off your old rocking horse . . . ' She snorted helplessly, her shoulders heaving, while Terry regarded her sourly.

'Go back to bed,' he told her.

'Now you know how I felt when you walked into the bathroom that day,' she told him. 'I'm sorry, Terry, but . . . '

Suddenly his own sense of humour began to surface as he regarded his bandaged ankle.

'I suppose it is funny,' he agreed, and began to laugh.

'Oh, don't!' she pleaded. 'Don't make me laugh again.'

'You'd better not make a noise,' he hissed. 'Eleanor will wonder what you're doing in my room, especially with Pamela away.'

Rosemary sobered immediately as she sat back on her knees. She was conscious that she wore her own delicate silk pyjamas instead of Army regulation stripes, and that Terry, too, was scantily clothed. It was the first time in her life that she had been in a man's bedroom.

Terry leaned forward and kissed her cheek.

'That's for being a true Florence Nightingale and fixing me up,' he said, then he bent down and kissed her lips. 'And that's for being yourself. We can't not be friends now!'

She flushed but did not look away.

⋆　⋆　⋆

Nancy was losing weight. She was eating hurried meals and working too hard, but it was the only way she knew to help an aching heart. She should not have run out on Jonathan that evening. She should have stayed and somehow made him understand that Greg Hamilton would never take his place in her life. She had impressed that on Greg at their next meeting.

She should have reasoned with

Jonathan instead of leaving him. He would soon have seen that he was making a mistake. He would have rumpled her hair, then pulled her into his arms.

'It's good to be home, duchess!'

'Don't call me duchess. I keep telling you . . . Rover!'

He would playfully grab her when she called him Rover because he was a newshound and roved about so much.

'You make me sound like a dog,' he would complain.

'And you make me sound like someone out of 'Alice In Wonderland.' '

'You look like Alice, with your soft fair hair. You seem such a child at times, my Nancy.'

'But I'm not a child,' she would whisper, and he would pull her into his arms, kissing her passionately.

When Nancy remembered those moments, she could feel the harsh sobs beginning to rise in her throat, and she would weep until she was tired. Greg had been posted overseas and Nancy's reaction had been bitter-sweet. She had missed the companionship he had offered, but she could put his place in her life into perspective, and she encouraged him to do the same.

She volunteered for overseas service with ENSA, and in the autumn of 1941 she found herself travelling to Gibraltar in cramped conditions aboard a military aircraft, then on to Cairo, where she was scheduled to entertain the troops and to broadcast a request programme, linking servicemen with their loved ones back home.

Soon her lovely voice was becoming known to millions as she sang requests from servicemen to their loved ones at home and from women to their husbands serving overseas.

Jonathan was about to return home early in December, but all else was forgotten when the Japanese attacked Pearl Harbour. His reports home were read avidly as he caught the high emotional drama of all that was happening, and Jonathan himself became deeply involved.

He came home feeling emotionally drained, and it was almost like a physical blow to find the flat empty and to remember that he and Nancy had parted in anger.

Jonathan slept round the clock, then went to see Geraldine.

His mother-in-law did not look her usual sparkling self. Richard had been gone longer than usual and she longed for him, yet was almost afraid to have him home again in case there was any more disappointment between them.

She was delighted to see Jonathan and welcomed him warmly.

'We're all so proud of Nancy,' she told him, 'as I expect you are, too. She's broadcasting request programmes from Cairo. It's a very popular programme.'

'I've been away,' Jonathan said. 'I'm just catching up on everything now that I'm home again. Nancy and I — we parted in anger. I don't even know if she wants to see me again!'

'Oh, Jonathan!' Geraldine was distressed. She'd seen Nancy before she left for Cairo, but her daughter hadn't confided in her. She, herself, had been rather withdrawn, she remembered. She had not encouraged Nancy to talk to her. Now she could not, in truth, tell Jonathan anything about Nancy's feelings except to offer him what comfort she could.

'I have to travel such a lot,' he was saying. 'I have to leave her, just when we're building up a good relationship. There's one great big casualty list of this war which isn't reported weekly — the number of hearts which are broken or bruised, and the emotions which are torn apart, because we can no longer be with our wives and sweethearts all the time.' He sighed.

'Oh, Jonathan, dear, you're so right,' Geraldine said. 'But if our country's worth fighting for, then our happiness is worth fighting for, too. We can't enjoy all the glory of living in a free country if we put ourselves in prison. Don't give up trying to put things right with Nancy, dear, if you love her.'

'I love her,' Jonathan said simply.

'Where are you going now?'

'I'm attached to an Army unit in Kent. I return there tomorrow.'

'Come and see me again when you return to London.' Geraldine said, kissing him. She had never loved her son-in-law more.

★ ★ ★

Nancy had written to Jonathan but she had received no reply and she knew that his letters often followed him around. The days had passed and soon it would be Christmas. That was always a special time for her and Jonathan. It was unthinkable that there should be any rift between them at Christmas time.

She leafed over her requests, thinking about all those other people who were apart and who sent messages of love to one another through the songs she sang. If they had quarrels and misunderstandings, then surely all was forgotten as she joined the thoughts of loved ones, one with another, even for a few minutes. Surely those few moments would keep their love warm for a long time to come.

Nancy looked at the messages, then her eyes began to glow a little as she took up her pen and added one more request.

From Duchess to Rover. This is a very special song which comes to you with all my love . . .

Nancy fitted the special request into the end of her programme. Perhaps Jonathan would hear it somewhere. If only he were back in England, listening . . .

'I'm Yours . . .'

Jonathan was back in camp. He had heard Nancy's broadcasts only once and the warmth of her voice over the air had cut deeply into his heart, yet he felt compelled to listen.

In the Officers' mess the radio was blaring forth, giving news bulletins interspersed with happy programmes and comedy shows designed to cheer up the Forces.

Jonathan ate a rather solitary meal, then suddenly Nancy's request programme was again on the air. Avidly he listened to the sound of her voice feeling, almost, that she was in the room with him. He could picture her so clearly, seeing her fresh beauty and the love in her eyes as she looked at him — had looked at him. On the last occasion, he had only seen the hurt in her.

Suddenly he could stand it no longer. His food had grown cold as he listened, and he pushed the remains of it away, forgetting his own hard and fast rule to always eat it up to the last crumb.

Jonathan rose abruptly, nodding to one or two of the officers, then he walked through to the bar, where he could no longer hear the radio. He sat in the bar of the Officers' Mess feeling more depressed than ever before in his life. There was laughter and conversation all around him, but he didn't feel part of it. From the canteen he could hear the faint notes of music, but he could no longer bear to listen to Nancy.

One of the officers came into the bar, smiling cheerfully as he came to sit beside Jonathan.

'Hello, Dukey,' he said. 'You look down in the mouth. What'll you have?'

'Got all I want, thanks,' Jonathan told him, lifting his glass. He felt decidedly anti-social, but he liked Steven Hawke — Sparrow to his friends — and he shuffled his stool into a better position to make room for him.

'I've just been saying to old Whitey that we chaps had better establish our positions before the place starts swarming with Yanks, now that America is in the war,' the officer said.

Jonathan sighed and smiled a little. 'No need for you to worry, Sparrow,' he said. 'A handsome chap like you has plenty of girls falling for you.'

'You've restored my self-esteem.' He grinned. 'But I'll have to ask you to stop calling me Sparrow and revert to Steven. It's my beak of a nose that does it. Girls tend to laugh. That reminds me, Dukey, someone else calls his missus 'Duchess.' It reminded me of you when I heard Nancy Wyllie saying that. She's singing a request from 'Duchess to Rover'. I've heard you calling your wife Duchess on the telephone.'

'Calling who?' Jonathan asked, his mind half on the conversation.

'Duchess. Duchess to Rover.'

'Rover? What Rover?' Jonathan's

mind began to clear a little. 'Rover,' he repeated, 'Duchess to ROVER!'

Suddenly he was on his feet and running through to the canteen.

Nancy had given careful thought to her special song for Jonathan and had chosen to sing, 'You'll Never Know Just How Much I Love You.' It was her own favourite, and popular with her audience who had joined in to sing it with her.

But for once she was singing only for one person, and something in the quality of her voice seemed to communicate itself to the audience so that they grew quiet as she began to sing it through once again.

You'll never know just how much
  I love you,
You'll never know just how much
  I care,
And if I tried . . .

Jonathan's face was white as he listened intently.

You ought to know for haven't I
  told you so,
A million or more times,
You went away and my heart
  went with you.

Suddenly he was aware that his cheeks were wet with tears as he knew that Nancy was singing only for him.

If there is some other way to
  prove that I love you,
I swear I don't know how,
You'll never know if you don't
  know now.

The last notes died away to thunderous applause and several men in the Officers' Mess looked curiously at the hard-bitten war correspondent who often seemed to be made of india-rubber. He had turned away and was wiping his face with his handkerchief.

'Are you OK, Duke?' one asked.

He nodded, unable to speak for a moment. 'Just got a letter to write,' he croaked, and made for the desk in his room. If he didn't write now, while his heart was full, he would not be able to match Nancy in complete and open honesty between them. He wrote from his heart, and posted the letter as soon as it was penned.

★　★　★

How time passed, thought Eleanor, as the summer of 1942 moved into autumn, then winter. In August she listened to the sad news of the loss of the Duke of Kent, and in November the Allies landed in North-West Africa. However, by the summer of 1943, the Allies had started to push forward in Libya.

Eleanor only received an occasional letter from Paul, but these she read avidly, over and over again. He could express the affection between them on paper much more easily than on the occasions when they talked together, and she was very much aware of the uncertainty with which he regarded the future.

Terry had spent an extended leave at home after he had injured his ankle, and he and Rosemary had become close friends.

Eleanor could not help contrasting the frank open pleasure which her brother showed in his growing love for Rosemary Archer with the quiet shyness of Paul, yet she loved this in him.

Every day the post brought letters for Eleanor from all parts of the country and abroad, and if the postman was late, she was often at the door to meet him before leaving for school in the morning.

'None from your young man today, Miss Wyllie,' Tom McFadyen would say. 'One from London — that's probably your mother — and two for the young lady officer.'

Eleanor was always glad to hear from her mother, even though she said little about her personal affairs.

Nancy was here the other evening,

she wrote. *She's back in London for a few weeks, but I think she's eating her heart out for Jonathan who is with the Eighth Army and writing splendid reports about their advance on Rommel. She may be going overseas with ENSA again soon.*

Nancy hadn't mentioned this in her last letter, Eleanor mused.

In that letter Nancy had been concerned for their mother who talked so little about Richard these days. Eleanor scanned the letter for mention of his name, but found none.

I met Maria Fischer in London the other day, her mother continued. *She was full of life and enjoying her work. Perhaps she'll come to see you some time at Fairlaw. Terry still appears to delight in his friendship with Rosemary Archer. I have suggested he brings her to see me some time, if it can be arranged.*

Eleanor laid aside her mother's letter. Geraldine's writing was now more careful than it had been at one time, but the sparkle had gone. Nancy was quite right. Their mother was not truly happy. Something was troubling her deeply.

Eleanor sighed then went to leave the two letters for Rosemary on the hall table. They were both in Terry's handwriting.

Terry was now attached to RAF Bomber Command, organising heavy raids on the Ruhr, Berlin and Cherbourg. By the end of January 1943 the use of radar was more widespread, and Terry found this very exciting. In fact, he found everything exciting now that Rosemary Archer occupied such a firm place in his heart.

* * *

For Geraldine the days were passing in a hazy round of hard work and coping with rationing and shortages. She hadn't been able to throw off her doubts and confusion as to the way her life was shaping.

Had she been impulsive when she married Richard, she wondered.

He had mixed with famous people, been lauded and applauded, and had provided music, laughter and entertainment for countless hundreds of people almost every night of his life. They were exactly the same age, she and Richard, but her spirit had grown old under the weight of her responsibilities, whilst his had remained young.

When he came home on leave, his legs could carry him upstairs two at a time, whilst she had to slow down a little in her step. She examined her face for tired skin and wrinkles and was surprised sometimes that she had not aged more than she expected. The heaviness was inside herself, not on the outside.

By the summer of 1943 Geraldine began to feel brighter as the bombing raids lessened and the casualties in shipping were less than they had been for some time.

Soon Richard would be home again

on leave, and she could arrange her own time off to suit. Perhaps they could recapture some of the old magic once again.

One evening, a few weeks later, the phone rang, and a cheerful voice asked for Lieutenant-Commander Ransome.

'He's away at the moment,' Geraldine told the caller. 'I expect him home on leave fairly soon.'

'Is that Mrs Ransome?'

'Yes.'

'This is Lieutenant Gilvray . . . Kenneth Gilvray. I expect you'll be having Lieutenant-Commander Ransome home sooner than you think, ma'am. He's my superior officer, and I'm speaking from Sheffield. He's probably just been delayed for a day or two, but we docked at Portsmouth on Wednesday. Could you tell him Eileen has had our baby and it's a boy? We're going to call him Richard.'

'Oh, how lovely!' Geraldine exclaimed. 'I'm sure my husband will be delighted, too. I'll tell him just as soon as he arrives home. Congratulations to you and your wife, Lieutenant Gilvray.'

'Thank you, Mrs Ransome.'

Geraldine put down the telephone with a lightness of heart she had not experienced for some time. When would Richard arrive?

She wrote down the message in case the name slipped her mind, also the telephone number of Lieutenant Gilvray's home, and placed it on Richard's desk, then she went to check up on her food store. He liked home-made ginger biscuits and she might have just enough ingredients to make a batch. Humming happily, Geraldine went to work.

A week later Geraldine ate the last of the biscuits, though they tasted like sawdust in her mouth.

Had he been recalled suddenly, she wondered. But if so, why hadn't he telephoned? She herself had telephoned a number he had once given her, but she was told that there was no information available. For a while she debated on whether she should telephone Lieutenant Gilvray on some pretext but ... but suppose Richard had merely chosen not to come home?

Geraldine had spent another week debating the point, then she rang the number Lieutenant Gilvray had given her. A woman answered and told her that Lieutenant Gilvray had now gone back off leave.

'I ... I only wanted your address to send a christening gift for the baby,' Geraldine said, with perfect honesty since she had already bought a silver napkin ring. 'This is Mrs Ransome. How is the baby?'

'Making excellent progress. I'm Ellen's mother, Mrs Ransome.'

Geraldine copied down the address then put down the telephone shakily. It was true then. Richard had not come home, yet he had been on leave in Portsmouth. Slowly she began to contemplate the fact that her marriage might be finished.

$\star$ $\star$ $\star$

Eleanor was also getting through the days with a heavy heart. Often there would be a gap between Paul's letters, then she would receive a batch of them which she enoyed reading according to date. But the weeks were passing into months, and she had not heard from Paul.

Then she came home one evening to find a message waiting for her to ring Paul's father at a number in Ayr. Eleanor went cold. If anything had happened to Paul, his father was the next of kin . . .

Jenny watched with silent sympathy as Eleanor threw off her coat and rushed to the telephone. Unashamedly Jenny listened to Eleanor's end of the conversation.

'I see . . . a military hospital near Plymouth. Don't worry, I'll go straightaway. Yes, I'll telephone you as soon as I've seen him, Mr Bryden.'

Eleanor finished her conversation

then turned to Jenny as she hung up the receiver. Her face was white but there was purpose in her manner.

'Paul's in hospital in Plymouth, Jenny,' she said. 'He's been wounded in action, but Mr Bryden has had no details of the extent of his injuries. I must leave for Plymouth straight-away.'

'But, Miss Eleanor!' Jenny's eyes opened wide. 'What about your job, and the Red Cross?'

'I'll soon get someone to take my place at school. I'll go round now and see Mr Johnstone, the headmaster, about finding someone to take over my class for a little while. Goodness knows I've done plenty of relief work myself. And as for the Red Cross, Monica Osborne can do that.' She spoke in breathless staccato bursts.

'I'll have to pack a bag quickly, Jenny. I might even have to travel to Edinburgh to try to get a seat on the train. There are such great long queues these days. And I must try to get a seat.

You can hold the fort for me, can't you, Jenny?'

'Don't worry about a thing, Miss Eleanor,' she said. 'I'll take care of everything for you. What do I say to Mrs Geraldine if she telephones?'

'Tell her exactly what has happened, of course,' Eleanor said briskly. 'Paul Bryden has been wounded, and I'm going to see him.'

It was a long, nightmare journey to Plymouth. The train seemed to spend hours in some stations without any apparent reason, then at other stations everyone was asked to change trains.

Tired and weary, Eleanor at first tried in vain to find hotel accommodation in Plymouth, then decided to leave her bags in 'Left Luggage' before going to the hospital without any more waste of time. She washed her hands and face in the waiting-room at the station, though she still felt travel stained.

Paul's arm and shoulder were in plaster and there was a pad taped down with sticking plaster above his right eye.

His face was thin and pale, and he stared with astonishment, then sheer wonder and delight when he saw Eleanor walking into the ward.

'How did you know?' he asked, after she bent to kiss him.

'Your father told me. He couldn't travel himself, but I've promised to keep him informed.'

'But how did you manage to get away?'

'I just came,' Eleanor said simply. 'I just caught the train and here I am. I'll find accommodation somewhere, and be with you for a few days.'

His eyes were almost feverish in their brightness.

'My right arm and shoulder are wounded,' he said. 'Though I was very lucky with the head wound. It could so easily have been my eyes . . . '

'Oh, Paul!' she whispered. 'Don't even think about that. Just think about getting better.'

'It's my writing hand,' he said quietly.

A moment later a nurse bustled

264

forward, and Paul was given an injection which soon made him very sleepy. Eleanor had taken hold of his hand.

'It could be a handicap,' he whispered.

'We'll see that it isn't!'

'I was always afraid of this, darling,' he told her. 'I was always afraid to love you . . . '

The last words were like a sigh and she was unsure whether she had heard correctly, but Eleanor was quite determined on one thing. She would stay with Paul until she was sure he was on the way to recovery, then she would arrange for him to go to Fairlaw for convalescence.

If he really did love her, then nothing was going to come between them, not even his injuries. She wouldn't let Paul go.

★   ★   ★

It was some time, however, before Paul could be moved, and Eleanor returned to Fairlaw to face yet another war-time winter.

In January 1944 General Eisenhower took over as Commander-in-Chief of the Allies, and Terry had something even more exciting to think about. Early in January there was news of a new jet-propelled aircraft which was going into production and he was enthralled and excited about it.

He was going to be busy for some time, he reflected, and it was time he sorted out his private life. As soon as he could arrange leave for himself, he travelled north to see Rosemary.

Eleanor could not have wished for a better time to have Terry come home on leave. At last, after weeks of waiting and two visits to Plymouth, Paul Bryden had been well enough to travel to Fairlaw for convalescence.

When he arrived, however, he had looked so pale and exhausted after the journey that Eleanor insisted on bed-rest. She was very worried about him and welcomed her brother's arrival with open arms.

'I hope you've got a long leave, Terry,' she said.

'Seven days. Where's Rosemary?'

'On duty, of course. She'll be home just after seven. Oh, Terry, I've got Paul here as well. He was wounded, you know, but he's convalescing now. He thinks he'll be OK in a day or two and that it was only the journey, but I'm worried that it's more than that.'

'I'll go and see Paul then — see if he wants anything. But you might as well know, I'm here to see Rosemary. It's important. Wish me luck, Eleanor.'

'I do,' she assured him, meeting his gaze clearly.

Paul looked better after Terry had helped him have a bath.

'I feel great,' he told Eleanor. 'After a good night's sleep, I'll be able to cope by myself. There'll be no need to bother Terry again.'

'We'll see how you are tomorrow.' Eleanor smiled. 'How's the arm?'

Paul's face sobered a little. 'Ah . . . that's a little bit different. I think I'll have to grow a beard. My fingers are still almost completely stiff.'

'Have a beard by all means,' she told him, 'but we're going to work on those fingers, you and I. We won't allow them to win. I'll find you a small rubber exercise ball.'

Paul looked at his injured hand and arm. It seemed a long time since he had taken his right arm for granted. But now he'd had to allow Terry Wyllie to shave him.

★ ★ ★

Rosemary was tired when she came off duty. The early anti-aircraft battery had grown into a major unit, and she was kept very busy. Pamela Bishop had married her fiancé, Bob Taylor, the previous September, and had now been posted to Hampshire. Rosemary missed her, but she was well liked by the other officers, and had many other friends.

Terry was alone in the lounge when Rosemary walked in, going as usual to look for letters on the hall table.

'No letter today, darling.' Terry's voice reached her from the semi-darkness of the lounge, and her heart leaped. 'I came myself instead,' he added.

'Terry!' she cried. 'Terry, you're home!'

She ran forward, and suddenly she was in his arms and he was kissing her fiercely, then leading her forward to sit down on the settee in front of the glowing fire.

'I had to come and see you, my darling,' he told her. 'I'm going to be very busy now. The war is definitely turning in our favour and everyone is going to be needed to make the final push. There are great, exciting times ahead, but I must know that I have you as part of my life for the future.'

The softness of a wall-light fell on his face and Rosemary stared at him. Of course she loved him, every line of his face, every change of expression, every crinkle of laughter in him, was a delight to her.

'Let me buy you a ring,' he pleaded. 'I'm willing to make it an engagement, not a wedding, until you feel ready to marry me. That's how much I love you. But I want to know you're mine, Rosemary. I've got to know where I stand.'

'I'm yours,' she said simply. 'I'll be proud and very happy to wear your ring.'

He drew her into his arms, kissing her soft lips and running a hand over her smooth black hair. Her eyes glowed like sapphires in the soft lights.

'You're very precious to me, Rosemary,' he said huskily.

'I'm so happy,' she confessed. 'Could we have an engagement party? Some of the girls would like to come, I'm sure. What about your mother and Nancy, and other friends?'

'I'll ring up one or two chaps. Of course we'll have a party. Eleanor will love it, and Jenny, even if she grumbles about rations. Oh, Rosemary, for once my heart is at ease, now that we're engaged.'

'Better than last time, with Maria?' She couldn't help the question, even as she bit her lip, wishing she hadn't asked. 'Sorry, I shouldn't have said that.'

'No, it's better that you should know,' Terry told her. 'Maria and I were very young and thought ourselves in love. I think we were. But there was more excitement than contentment. Maria always said we weren't right for one another. She could see the future more clearly than I could. We're still friends, you know.'

'I know, darling. I'm just jealous. Should we invite Maria to our engagement party? Would she like that?'

'She would love it,' Terry assured her. 'She's met someone else herself, you know. He's Austrian. He's playing the violin in one of our big orchestras, having been naturalised before the war.

Maria can't travel freely, but she can come up to Fairlaw if she reports to the police. I'm sure it can be arranged.'

Maria was delighted with her invitation and telephoned immediately to say that she was arranging time off and would be able to travel on the day of the party.

'She can have the small room over the porch,' Eleanor said. 'It used to be hers anyway. Can you come in with me, Rosemary, then Mother can have her old room, and Nancy will share with her? She won't mind Paul having her room. Richard is somewhere on the Atlantic and Jonathan could be anywhere.'

Nancy travelled north on her own after a recording session. Geraldine was already at Hillcrest, having managed to arrange a week off from her job. Eleanor scrutinised her mother carefully. Apart from one or two grey hairs, Geraldine looked the same as ever. She was still slender, and her dress looked pretty for the party.

'You look super, Mother,' she said. 'You never change.'

'Don't I?' Geraldine asked quickly, and there was something urgent in the question.

'No, you don't,' Eleanor said sincerely, 'not in looks, anyway. No need to do anything, by the way. Rosemary and I have coped. She's nice, isn't she?'

'She's lovely,' Geraldine agreed. 'We must get to know one another better. I'm glad Maria's coming, too.'

'She should be here any time now,' Eleanor said, glancing at the clock. 'I meant to send one of Terry's friends to the station, but I forgot. Anyway, she knows the way.'

Maria didn't turn up after all.

The Power Of Love

It was after two in the morning when the London train finally dropped Maria at Fairlaw Station. There had been a bombing raid somewhere in the Midlands, and the train had been held up for hours. The party would now be over, Maria thought, as she hurried to Hillcrest. She felt almost sick with disappointment and fatigue as she clutched her overnight bag, and stumbled through the semi-darkness.

At Hillcrest all was in darkness, but Maria remembered the pantry window. No need to disturb anyone. She would squeeze through it and sleep in a chair till morning. The pantry was at the end of a stone passage, and as Maria tiptoed towards the kitchen, something stopped her in her tracks. Surely she could smell burning?

Hurrying, she pushed open the

lounge door, to be met by flames shooting to the ceiling. No-one heard Maria's scream of horror when she saw that the drawing-room was ablaze.

Swiftly she closed the door, then rushed upstairs to wake the household, banging loudly on the old dinner gong which she had picked up from the hall.

Despite her efforts, the heavy smoke was already filling the hall and stairs, and Geraldine could smell it immediately she woke up. Her room was directly above the drawing-room and Maria, knowing the geography of the house, rushed there first of all.

'Fire!' she shouted. 'Mrs Wyllie . . . I mean Mrs Ransome . . . you must get up. Nancy! Outside for everybody! Fire in the drawing-room!'

Geraldine's head reeled and she felt rather sick and giddy, but already the household was well awake and Nancy was struggling into her dressing-gown.

'Come on, Mother,' she said, her eyes wide with shock and fright. 'It . . . it's fire all right. I can smell the smoke.'

Geraldine was now wide awake and Nancy helped her to put on her dressing-gown. A moment later they heard Terry running past the door and racing to the telephone.

Eleanor and Rosemary also appeared in the bedroom, both girls white faced with fear as they helped Geraldine to the back stairs which were farther away from the fire.

'Paul!' Eleanor cried. 'Where's Paul? He's sleeping in Nancy's room. Here, Nancy, see to Mother and I'll check up . . . '

She was gone in a flash, but already Paul was stumbling towards them, the smoke now choking them as they ran down the stairs.

In the meantime, Maria had made her way to Jenny's rooms above the kitchen.

'Mercy on us!' the old woman cried. 'What's the commotion? Oh, so it's you, Miss Maria. You got here then . . . '

'Fire!' Maria exclaimed. 'Get up, Jenny. Here, put on your robe. I'll help you. It's fire in the main part of the house, and you must get outside. Terry has telephoned for the Fire Brigade.'

Outside in the cool night air Eleanor was standing a little apart from the others.

'It was my fault,' she whispered. 'I should have checked that the drawing-room was safe.'

'It was nobody's fault,' Paul assured her, coming to put his arm round her. 'Don't start blaming yourself, Eleanor.'

The worst casualty was Maria, who had lost her voice, having breathed more than her share of smoke, and whose hand was being treated for burns.

'We owe our lives to her,' Eleanor acknowledged. She could not bear to think what might have happened otherwise.

'We owe you a debt we can never repay,' Geraldine told her sincerely as she came to sit with Maria, who had been ordered to bed for a day or two.

'Such nonsense! It is I who owe this

family so much,' Maria croaked. 'If it had not been for Terry, I wouldn't have got out of Germany and you all made me so welcome during those difficult first few weeks. And I am glad Terry is happy with his pretty girl. She is very good looking, no?'

'And so are you, my dear,' Geraldine said, kissing her. 'I'm delighted that you've made a good life for yourself.'

'Some day Anton, who is to be my husband, will go back to Germany with me when the Nazis have been driven out. Some day all will be peace.'

Maria's black eyes were full of dreams and Geraldine smiled.

'It's good to look forward, Maria,' she said, then she sighed as she left the room. Sometimes she, herself, was afraid to look forward.

★ ★ ★

Nancy had engagements in London and had to leave the following day. Terry also had to rejoin his unit and it was left to Eleanor and Paul to start cleaning up the mess.

Nancy was glad that she would have a night's rest before going to the studios in the morning. She let herself into the flat and automatically bent to pick up any post, but there was none on the hall floor. A moment later she heard a small sound in the living-room and the smell of Jonathan's pipe wafted out to her. For a long moment she felt almost powerless to move; it had been so long since they had seen each other. Then the door flew open and he was there, facing her. He wore one of her flowered aprons and his sleeves were rolled up.

'Hello, Duchess,' he said huskily, and held out his arms. A moment later Nancy was clinging to him, unable to check the tears which coursed down her cheeks.

'You smell of train,' he said, burying his nose in her hair.

'I smell of smoke, and fire,' she told him. 'Between us we almost burned the house down. Eleanor blames herself, but we were all careless.'

'I want to hear everything you've been doing, day by day, since I last saw you.' He guided her into the living-room. 'By the way, I'm making supper. Is dried egg and tinned beans OK?'

'Anything,' Nancy said happily. 'Anything at all. It will taste like nectar.'

'Whatever you say, Duchess. I suppose I can call you Duchess now, since you announced it to the world.'

'Oh, Jonathan, I didn't know if you would hear it, but it was a chance I had to take. Oh, darling . . . suppose you hadn't heard it . . . '

Later, clean and refreshed, she lay in Jonathan's arms whilst he told her many stories about his assignments.

'I've only got two or three days at home, darling. I suspect there's something big in the wind. I think we'll be making the final push.'

'Landing in France, you mean?'

'Ssh!' he said. 'That would be top secret, but if my judgment is correct, then it has to come.'

'I'll be so glad when it's all over, darling.'

'Now that I've got you, so will I,' he told her.

★ ★ ★

Geraldine and Maria travelled back to London together. Maria had been forced to spend a few more days at Hillcrest because of her burns, but already she was feeling much better and the news was such that both she and Geraldine were keen to get back to duty. From all fronts it seemed that the war was turning in favour of the Allies.

On June 6, 1944, the Allies landed in France.

Each day the news was better and better as the Allies advanced into France. Geraldine returned to her job, working hard for long hours and very glad to be part of her team doing their bit.

But as the summer of 1944 moved into autumn, a new horror opened up for her as the V1 and V2 attacks began. For her there was something eerily unreal about the unmanned rockets which were bringing new destruction, and her work became even more important as they sought to pin-point the source of the rockets.

Then, one evening, as Geraldine climbed the stairs to her flat, the steps appeared to bounce up and down in front of her eyes. Surely a rocket had landed, her tired mind told her, and she had not heard the whine of it. But even as the thought entered her mind, all became black and she slid forward on to the stairs.

Nancy had tried to telephone, knowing that her mother should be home, but there was no reply. She had newly returned from a tour of duty in the Midlands and after a moment's deliberation, Nancy hurried round to the flat.

Geraldine had recovered from her faint and had managed to let herself into the flat, where she lay on the settee feeling sick and ill. Deep throbbing pains burned in her back and she felt powerless to help herself. From the mists of her pain she was aware that Nancy was beside her and was trying to make her comfortable.

'Lie still,' said Nancy. 'The doctor will be here shortly. I should have insisted on sending for him weeks ago.'

'I've probably twisted it.' Geraldine groaned. 'I thought I was just a little tired . . . '

'A little tired!'

The bell rang and a moment or two later Dr Lacey, a cheerful, competent man in his late fifties, was kneeling down beside Geraldine and examining her carefully.

'You say you've had the pain before, Mrs Ransome?' he asked, after he had taken her temperature and blood pressure.

'Only vaguely.'

'You busy ladies!' he admonished. 'You neglect yourselves far too much these days. I'm afraid it's hospital for you for a more thorough examination, but I think it will mean an operation.'

The following week was an anxious one for Eleanor and Nancy.

Geraldine's operation had been a success, but her recovery was slow. Now that she knew her fatigue and depression had had its root cause in physical illness, her mind had become clearer and some of the old Geraldine showed through as she encouraged Eleanor to go back home.

'Will you come home when you're free to travel to Fairlaw, and allow Jenny to spoil you?' Eleanor asked. 'We're still clearing up, but we can find you a cosy corner.'

'Perhaps,' her mother said. 'I can't make plans just yet.'

Eleanor travelled home next day and Paul met her at the station. He had a medical coming up in another two weeks, and he was so much improved that he expected to return to duty.

When she stepped off the London train and saw Paul walking towards her, his step buoyant and his arm swinging where he had once held it stiffly, she didn't try to hide her love for him, and he wrapped her tightly in his arms.

'I've missed you so much,' he told her, and her heart was warmed by his love. As they walked home from the station, Paul kept an arm round her.

'Would it be wrong of me to want to marry you?' he asked her. 'I shall have to make my way again after the war, and we would have to start at the bottom of the ladder. I keep asking myself if it's fair to you.'

'Oh, Paul!' Eleanor's eyes were like stars. 'It will be all over Fairlaw if we start kissing here in the street, but that's what I'd like to do. Of course I'll marry you. I've never wanted anything else. I nearly proposed to you myself since it's a Leap Year.'

'I love you so much, Eleanor,' Paul said. 'I've always thought that you deserve the best.'

'For me, you are the best.'

'But . . . but you're so beautiful,' Paul whispered. 'You could marry anybody.'

'I don't want to marry anybody, I want to marry you.' Eleanor smiled contentedly, happy in the knowledge that he loved her.

★ ★ ★

Commander Richard Ransome had never been so glad to see Portsmouth as his ship arrived back in port for repairs. It seemed years since he had been home.

On his last leave he had been required to stay aboard for a day or two, then to attend a debriefing along with his senior officer and friend, Captain Hugo Nelson, who had received a few minor wounds when their ship was shelled.

The captain, known as 'The Admiral' behind his back, had begun to feel the effects of his wounds while in Portsmouth and had required further treatment. Richard was reluctant to leave him on his own in Portsmouth, and had telephoned Geraldine to say he would be delayed for a day or two.

There had been no reply and somehow the days had passed so that Richard had not managed to get to London at all. He and Captain Nelson had spent a few quiet days together making sure 'The Admiral' was fit before returning to duty.

Later, Richard had learned from his junior officer, Lieutenant Gilvray, that he was now godfather to a new baby and that Geraldine had been asked to pass on the good news. Richard wrote her a letter which, on second reading, appeared to be full of excuses, so he tore it up. He would soon be home again — then he could tell her all about it.

But the war was taking a new turn as the Allies landed in France, and every ship was needed to keep the strength of the Navy at full pitch. Richard did his best to keep Geraldine informed and to reassure her that he was still OK.

Her own replies were not the free-flowing letters he once loved to receive, though — they were stilted, almost difficult letters, and sometimes Richard frowned as he read them. Why couldn't she try a little harder? What had happened to the happy, light-hearted woman he had married?

The flat was empty when he arrived home and there was a slight air of neglect about the place.

Richard opened a few tins and made himself a light supper, then his heart leaped when he heard a key in the door. As the door opened, Richard hurried through to the sitting-room, then paused when he saw Nancy standing there.

'Oh, Richard!' she cried, going to hug him. 'You're home! Oh, I'm so glad. Did you get my letter?'

'No, I've had no letter from you. Where did you send it?'

'I sent it to the address you gave us when you first joined the Navy.'

'Out of date now, Nancy,' Richard said, then his eyes sharpened. 'What was in the letter? Has something happened?'

'No . . . Well, yes, though it's OK now. Mother has been rather ill. She needed an operation but she's on the mend now, though still rather weak. It's a relief in a way. We'd all seen that she hadn't been herself for ages.'

'I . . . I see,' Richard said. Somehow the news was more devastating to him than many battles he had encountered.

'Sit down,' Nancy said gently. 'I'll get you a drink.'

'No, I must go to Geraldine,' Richard said hurriedly. Suddenly it seemed as though there was no time to lose.

'Five minutes won't make any difference. I'll come with you.'

'Where is she?' he asked.

'She's been moved to the Kingsley Park Nursing Home. We can get in to see her any time. We'll take a taxi, if we can find one.'

Geraldine was in a small, pleasant room on the first floor and for a moment she looked blankly at Richard as he and Nancy were escorted into the room. Then she gave a small cry of delight.

'Not very long, please,' the nurse told them. 'The patients will require to be settled for the night.'

But already Richard was striding to the bed and enfolding Geraldine in his arms.

She looked frail and delicate, but her eyes were as brilliant as ever and shining with tears as she looked at him.

'I'm so sorry, my darling,' he whispered tenderly. 'I didn't know you were ill or I'd have found some way to be with you.'

'There's no need to worry,' she told him. 'I'm on the mend now. Oh, Richard, darling, I'm so glad you've come.'

She put a hand up to his face, seeing that he now had a sprinkling of white hairs amongst the crisp curls, and that there were faint lines at the sides of his eyes. Suddenly Richard was a little older.

'You're very precious to me,' he told her huskily.

'Oh, Richard, darling, I'm better

already just to hear you say that,' she told him. 'I've missed you so. Have you a long leave?'

'Seven more days. Don't worry, I'll soon be home for good. You'll see. Let's look forward to that.' He held her frail body in his arms and kissed her gently.

★   ★   ★

There were few places more beautiful than Fairlaw in springtime, thought Geraldine, as she rested in an old chair under the beech tree in the garden. It was now two weeks since she had travelled up from London and the peace and quiet of Fairlaw was helping her to gather a little strength.

Eleanor crossed the lawn carrying a tray of coffee and biscuits.

'I thought we'd better snatch a few quiet moments while we can, Mummy,' she said, smiling. 'Tomorrow, the house will be bursting at the seams, between Paul's father and auntie, Rosemary's parents and all our family. Thank goodness the Glendower Hotel can take our overflow of guests.'

'Well, it isn't every week we have a double wedding,' Geraldine replied happily. 'It feels strange to be both the bride's mother and the bridegroom's on the same day.'

'Eighth of May. That was Granny's birthday,' Eleanor said. 'It was always a happy day at Fairlaw, even when we were small. I suppose that's why I chose it, though it was Rosemary's idea to have a double wedding. She's come to love it here so much and I think she knew how much it would please Terry. Are you sure you're OK, Mother?' Eleanor looked at her mother anxiously.

Geraldine had been very slow to pull round, then the surgeons had decided that a second operation was necessary. It had been an anxious time for all of them, but gradually Geraldine was beginning to gain a little strength. She still had a long way to go, thought Eleanor, biting her lip.

Geraldine avoided Eleanor's searching look.

'I'm fine, dear,' she assured her elder daughter.

'Would you prefer to have been in London, Mummy?' Eleanor asked.

'No, darling, not this time. I prefer to be right here where I am. I'm so happy for you and Rosemary — and Terry and Paul, we mustn't forget the men. You are happy, aren't you, Eleanor? Marriage isn't always easy and misunderstandings can brew up so easily, but if you're really in love they can soon be overcome.'

'Mummy, I can't begin to tell you how happy I am,' Eleanor said, and Geraldine nodded.

'Come away in now, Mrs Geraldine,' Jenny called. 'It's not high summer yet. You'll catch cold if you sit out too long, and you not at all robust yet.'

Geraldine smiled ruefully. Jenny must be obeyed.

'Come on, I'll help you.' Eleanor said, and put her strong young arm round her mother's slender waist.

Jenny was preparing a tray of tea for the guests when Richard arrived, accompanied by Nancy and Jonathan. Geraldine got up to welcome her husband, but he was there before her, holding her frail body in his arms.

She certainly needed to gain strength, he thought with inward concern, but already she had fought her way back on to her feet.

Geraldine looked at her tall husband who was so distinguished in his uniform and her pride showed in her eyes.

'You look marvellous, darling,' she said.

'So do you.' Then his voice lowered. 'How are you standing up to all the excitement?'

'It's giving me the boost I needed,' she assured him. 'It's going to be a help, not a hindrance. You'll see.'

★ ★ ★

On the morning of the wedding, everyone in the house gathered to listen to the voice of Winston Churchill telling the country that the war was over.

The whole of Fairlaw rang with bells, wedding bells mingling with the bells of victory.

The Glendower Hotel, where the reception was to be held, was full to overflowing with guests.

In spite of wartime austerity, this was one day in which everyone had done their bit towards making it a memorable and wonderful day. Tears were back in Geraldine's eyes when she saw the brides dressed in their wedding gowns. Her voice was husky as she hugged Eleanor, then Rosemary.

'You look beautiful, my darlings,' she said. 'I want you to know how proud I feel.'

'Thank you, Mummy,' Eleanor whispered, her eyes shining.

'I'm a very lucky girl,' Rosemary told her. 'Pamela says I'm only marrying

Terry to get myself a wonderful mother-in-law!'

Richard and Colonel Archer, both men smart and handsome in their uniforms, were giving the brides away.

Geraldine wore a beautiful suit of rose-gold silk, which brought a faint glow of warmth to her pale cheeks.

Friends of Eleanor's had decorated the church with flowers, paying tribute to a wonderful day in the country's history by choosing red tulips, white narcissi and the lovely blue of grape hyacinths. The flowers brought perfumed colour to the cool interior of the church, and the organ was playing softly when Geraldine arrived with Jonathan and Jenny.

Soon there was a rustle at the door of the church, and the organ began to play 'The Wedding March' as the bridal parties for the double wedding moved slowly down the aisle.

Geraldine's eyes were wet as she listened to the lovely words of the wedding service, then she and Mrs

Archer were called to the vestry to witness the signatures of the register, and to congratulate the two brides and 'grooms, all of them radiant with happiness.

Then the bridal party walked slowly out of the church and into the lovely sunshine, their happiness enhanced by the joy of victory.

★　★　★

It had been a long day, Geraldine thought that evening as she sat in the peace of the drawing-room at Hillcrest after everyone had gone to bed. Now that it was over she could relax, and her body trembled a little with weakness and fatigue. At least she had managed to get through the day.

Richard was locking up the house, and making it safe for the night. Geraldine looked into the remnants of the fire, thinking deeply about the past. Again she could see herself as a young wife arriving at Hillcrest with Laurence's protective arms about her.

How young they had been, and how they had loved one another.

She could see again the dignified but gracious lady who had been her mother-in-law, Constance Wyllie, and the stern upright figure of Stephen Wyllie, whom she had come to love as her own father.

From the shadows she could see the other people she had loved — her own parents, Aunt Margaret and Alex Kinloch who had been such a staunch friend. They all had a place here on this day in her memories, even as she gave thanks for the blessings and happiness of the present.

Her thoughts were also with her children; with Eleanor and Paul, Terry and his Rosemary. Nancy and Jonathan were returning to London in the morning, no doubt to be separated once more, but their love was now so strong that she was sure it could withstand any pressure.

'All locked up,' Richard said, coming into the room. 'How are you, my darling? I'd better get you to bed straightaway.'

'I was just sitting here, remembering,' Geraldine replied, as he helped her to her feet.

He folded her in his arms with his chin against her hair.

'It's nice to remember a little,' Richard murmured, 'but we're still too young to live on our memories.' He looked down into her face. 'My love, I promise you, the best is yet to come.'

THE END

We do hope that you have enjoyed reading this large print book.

Did you know that all of our titles are available for purchase?

We publish a wide range of high quality large print books including:
Romances, Mysteries, Classics
General Fiction
Non Fiction and Westerns

Special interest titles available in large print are:
The Little Oxford Dictionary
Music Book, Song Book
Hymn Book, Service Book

Also available from us courtesy of Oxford University Press:
Young Readers' Dictionary
(large print edition)
Young Readers' Thesaurus
(large print edition)

For further information or a free brochure, please contact us at:
Ulverscroft Large Print Books Ltd.,
The Green, Bradgate Road, Anstey,
Leicester, LE7 7FU, England.
Tel: (00 44) **0116 236 4325**
Fax: (00 44) **0116 234 0205**

VISIONS OF THE HEART

Christine Briscomb

When property developer Connor Grant contracted Natalie Jensen to landscape the grounds of his large country house near Ashley in South Australia, she was ecstatic. But then she discovered he was acquiring — and ripping apart — great swathes of the town. Her own mother's house and the hall where the drama group met were two of his targets. Natalie was desperate to stop Connor's plans — but she also had to fight the powerful attraction flowing between them.

DIVIDED LOYALTIES

Phyllis Demaine

When Heather's fiancé, Adrian, is offered a wonderful job in America their future seems rosy. However, Adrian's brother, Carl, a widower, asks for Heather's help with his small, deaf son. Help which, as a speech therapist, Heather is qualified to give. But things become complicated when Carl goes abroad on business and returns with Gisel, to whom his son takes an instant dislike. This puts Heather in the position of having to choose between the boy's happiness and her own.

ZABILLET OF THE SNOW

Catherine Darby

For Zabillet, a young peasant girl growing up in the tiny French village of Fromage in the mid-fourteenth century, a respectable marriage is the height of her parents' ambitions for her. But life is changing. Zabillet's love for a handsome shepherd is tested when she is invited to join the La Neige household, where her mistress, Lady Petronella, has plans for her grand-son, Benet. And over all broods the horror of the Great Death that claims all whom it touches.

PERILOUS JOURNEY

Caroline Joyce

After the execution of Charles I, Louisa's Royalist father considers it too dangerous for her to stay in England and arranges for her to go to the Isle of Man with Armand de la Tremouille, the nephew of the island's Royalist Governor. Their ship is boarded by Parliamentarians who plan to sail for Ireland, but a storm causes them to be shipwrecked on the Calf of Man. Magnus Stapleton, the Parliamentarian chief, becomes infatuated with Louisa, but she has fallen in love with Armand.

THE GYPSY'S RETURN

Sara Judge

After the death of her cruel father, Amy Keene's stepbrother and stepsister treated her just as badly. Amy had two friends, old Dr. Hilland and the washerwoman, Rosalind, with her fatherless child Becky. When Rosalind falls ill, Amy is entrusted with a letter to be given to Becky on her marriage. When the letter's contents are discovered, it causes Amy both mental and physical suffering and sets the seal of fate upon Rosalind's gypsy friend, Elias Jones.

WEB OF DECEIT

Margaret McDonagh

A good-looking man turned up on Louise's doorstep one day, introducing himself as Daniel Kinsella, an Australian friend of her brother-in-law, Greg. He said he had come to stay whilst he did some research — apparently Greg had written to her about it. Louise's initial reaction was to turn him away, but he was very persuasive. However, she was to discover that Daniel had bluffed his way into her life, and soon she found herself caught up in his dangerous mission.